The Bassist's Guide to Injury Management, Prevention and Better Health

Volume Two

by Randall Kertz, D.C.

ISBN 13: 978-1-912126-28-6

Acknowledgments

Special thanks to: Ariane Cap, John Clayton, Ed Friedland, Stuart Hamm, Chris Jisi, Chris Clemente, Dino Monoxelos, Chi-chi Nwanoku, John Patitucci, Stuart & Laura Clayton, and all who supported Volume One and this current volume. My never ending thanks.

Notice

This book is designed to be a companion to *The Bassist's Guide to Injury Management, Prevention & Better Health - Volume One*, and it is recommended that the reader have that reference available as Volume Two builds on the concepts introduced there.

Preface

Since *The Bassist's Guide to Injury Management, Prevention & Better Health - Volume One* was published, the response from the musicians' community in general and the bassist community in particular has been overwhelmingly positive and validating, with many telling me that it helped them not only identify and overcome challenges but that it saved careers. Thank you. That being said, there is still more work to do. So with gratitude and without further adieu, *The Bassist's Guide to Injury Management, Prevention & Better Health - Volume Two!*

CHAPTER ONE

Mind Games

In *The Bassist's Guide to Injury Management, Prevention & Better Health - Volume One,* we covered general topics related to bass playing and staying healthy for the short and long term. Digging in a little deeper here, we explore some issues that may be less common, but are no less important to the bassist.

Repetitive strain type injuries, such as tendonitis, are caused by repeating a task over and over again in a similar fashion, which can result in injury even under the best conditions, let alone if one is unaware of how their body is handling this repetition. Knowledge of one's technique on the instrument and of the pertinent anatomy required to perform this technique is key to helping to avoid this type of injury, as we addressed in Volume One and which will be reinforced in this volume.

There is also a mental component to everything that we do on the instrument, just as there is in our everyday lives, and how we process this can be of great benefit or detriment to our playing and to remaining injury free. By learning proper posture, positioning, and being mindful of one's approach to the instrument in a physical way from the beginning, we can incorporate and employ proper habits, and in this way avoid having to make major changes later to accommodate pain or discomfort. As one's proficiency and knowledge increase, and playing becomes more second nature, mechanics are often given less attention, and we are able to enjoy playing for its own sake and spend less time and attention on how we perform these basic tasks. As one practices new skills, as in the learning of a new language or an instrument, we internalize, or 'hardwire' them, as they become learned behavior. This happens through repetition and practice, as we form specialized sets of connections which allow the brain to perform a task rapidly and efficiently. In the case of playing an instrument, these connections translate into physical effort as the neural patterns in the brain become the physical action the muscles perform, for example, the fingers running scales on the fingerboard. After a while, the mental and physical become imperceptible from each other, and then it is not as easy to change one's technique by just moving a finger or two to avoid discomfort, as new motion must be learned, incorporated, and practiced to train the brain to substitute the new pattern or position for the old one which has been it's 'go-to' pattern or position, and the new motion now must override the old familiar pattern mentally and physically. This kind of activity has traditionally been associated with the term 'muscle memory', in which the body can repeat an activity without thinking about it, for example, playing scales physically and with minimal if any attention while watching television. This 'muscle memory' idea, while addressing the physical component, frequently excludes the part about the mental, neural pattern, which is what directly produces this physical activity, and which is why, without much effort, one can repeat these scale patterns literally with their eyes closed.

Why is this important? You repeat what you learn, and an awareness of this concept of the mental driving the physical gives one the power to understand and therefore change or avoid bad habits, through knowledge of the mechanisms of how the brain and body process action and performance. Not being aware of this concept can lead to new types of injury or pathology, as what physically should respond to treatment and get better can resist all efforts due to this mental conditioning and these patterns which can make one's physical responses seem random and uncontrollable, as in the case of focal dystonia, which will be addressed in the next chapter.

So by implementing proper posture, technique, and awareness, ideally when one is beginning to learn or become serious about playing an instrument, or by incorporating these concepts in small bite-size chunks as one progresses rather than trying to revamp one's whole style and technique later when one's neural patterns are more likely to resist through familiarity, we can instill and teach ourselves proper habits and patterns which will help us now and in the future, rather than having to unlearn bad habits later, thus hardwiring for success.

CHAPTER TWO

Help

More conditions commonly seen in bassists, what they mean and affect, along with treatment options.

BAKER'S CYST

A Baker's cyst, or popliteal cyst, presents with the following symptoms:

- swelling behind the knee
- knee pain, sometimes going down into the back of the leg, many times worsening after activity or standing for long periods of time
- stiffness and an inability to fully flex (bend) the knee

Baker's Cyst – What it is

A Baker's cyst is a fluid filled cyst, or sac of abnormal character containing fluid, that causes a bulge behind the knee. This is usually discovered by a feeling of tightness and discomfort behind the knee, which can feel worse when you bend (flex) or extend your knee, or during activity, including walking. While cysts can come and go with no explanation, a Baker's cyst is usually the result of a problem with the knee joint, for example arthritis or a tear in the cartilage. The name is derived from the occupation, as bakers would and still do bend over frequently to put things in and take things out of the oven, which puts extra pressure on and causes friction at the back of the knee area. Unlike other cysts, a Baker's cyst is always located behind the knee.

The fluid present in a cyst is called synovial fluid, which helps normally with swinging the leg and reducing friction between the moving parts of the knee.

Baker's Cyst – What to do

- get a proper diagnosis, which may include an ultrasound, x-ray, or MRI to rule out more serious problems such as a tumor or blood clot.
- if there is no pain, the problem may go away on its own as cysts can and frequently do. Generally speaking, the larger the cyst, and if one continues the offending activity, such as bending or squatting frequently or in some way damaging the knee, the less likely it will go away on its own.
- aspiration, a procedure in which fluid is drawn out through a needle by a physician, will sometimes be performed, but can be tricky and care must be exercised.
- cortisone injection may reduce inflammation, and is sometimes performed after aspiration to help prevent recurrence of the cyst.
- icing the area and wrapping with a bandage can help to reduce pain and swelling if the condition is not too serious.
- ultrasound, therapeutic not diagnostic, can help to reduce inflammation. Diagnostic ultrasound may be used to assist in an aspiration or cortisone injection.
- surgery may be necessary, especially if the cause of the cyst is found to be a cartilage tear, causing the fluid build-up.
- reducing one's activity, RICE (rest, ice, compression, elevation), and over the counter anti-inflammatories can also help if safe for one to take. As usual consult your physician if unsure and never take more than the recommended amount.

BASAL JOINT ARTHRITIS

Basal joint arthritis, or arthritis of the thumb, presents with the following symptoms:

- pain at the base of the thumb, especially during pinching, gripping, or in extension, such as in the "thumbs up" position. This results in one experiencing weakness during pinching, or pain and weakness in extension.

Basal Joint Arthritis – What it is

Basal joint arthritis is the result of the wearing away of cartilage in the joint (place where two bones meet separated by cartilage) at the base of the thumb. The basal joint allows your thumb to move around so that you can perform small fine tasks. When this cushioning cartilage wears away, the bones of the joint become rough and grind on each other with motion, this causing more damage to the joint there. The first sign of this arthritis is pain, tenderness, and or stiffness in the thumb. It is felt at the base of the thumb as one tries to grip, pinch, or clasp something between the thumb and index fingers. I have commonly seen this condition in my office in dentists as well as instrumentalists. Pain can also occur from such everyday tasks as turning a door handle, a key in a lock, or snapping the fingers. Slap style bassists may also notice this condition more.

Pain and inflammation will cause one to have less strength and motion in the affected hand as the condition progresses. Everyday actions such as those already mentioned as well as opening jars, holding a drink, fastening buttons and working zippers can be affected due to pain and/or weakness occurring from the pain. Swelling at the base of the thumb may occur, or a bump may develop, both at the base of the thumb, and it will appear larger and swollen.

Basal Joint Arthritis – What to do

- The primary thing one can do from a prevention perspective is to be aware of the problem. One may see their physician and/or health care provider, and the most important thing they can do is to give a proper diagnosis, which is many times best demonstrated through an x-ray. I have seen this issue in bassists, and by educating them as to what the problem is and by having them avoid extension as much as possible by limiting that motion in the thumb, many times the condition will settle down and the pt. will be able to go back to normal activity. One can usually figure out ways to accomplish tasks and to play without the extra pressure and extreme ranges of motion they once used, and the issue improves. The condition itself will not go away completely, as once degeneration is present this part of the condition will not improve, but the symptoms can.
- Also as part of this awareness, it is up to the pt. to avoid clenching their hands into fists, gripping objects with greater pressure than necessary, and needlessly "checking" their thumb frequently throughout the day to see "if it is better", all of which will place extra demands on the joint and produce pain.
- Ice at the base of the thumb can help with pain temporarily and reduce inflammation.
- Anti-inflammatory medication can help with inflammation, as the name implies.
- Ultrasound applied to the base of the thumb can be helpful for inflammation.
- Acupuncture can help with pain relief.
- A corticosteroid injection can help with pain and inflammation if conservative methods fail, but without modifications of lifestyle and movement this will not be a lasting measure.
- One can learn to limit their range of motion in extension by wearing a splint, which will help to make the new decreased motion a habit.
- Glucosamine can help to keep cartilage from degenerating further by delivering a water molecule to the cartilage, which helps to hydrate it and thereby slow the degenerative process.
- Surgery can be an option, best considered only if all other methods fail.

DEQUERVAIN'S SYNDROME, OR TENOSYNOVITIS

DeQuervain's Syndrome, or tenosynovitis, will present with the following symptoms:

- pain at the base of the thumb caused and accompanied by inflammation, and felt with most thumb movement.

DeQuervain's Syndrome – What it is

DeQuervain's syndrome is pain that affects the thumb and the place where the thumb attaches to the rest of the hand, and is felt most during twisting movements, either with one's instrument or in everyday tasks. These movements include turning the hand towards the pinky, reaching the thumb under the hand towards the pinky, moving the hand and/or wrist sideways towards the pinky side of the hand (ulnar deviation), or with any forceful gripping, pinching, squeezing, or grasping. There are two tendon groups (tendons connect muscle to bone), called the abductors and the extensors, which control the thumb, pulling the thumb outward and away from the hand, as is seen many times in bowing techniques on string instruments. These tendons, specifically the abductor pollicis longus and the extensor pollicis brevis, pass through a tunnel, or compartment on the side of the wrist above the thumb. When overuse causes inflammation of a tendon, you have tendonitis, a condition described earlier in this chapter, and this causes pain in that area. Fluid, designed to allow the tendons to slide easily, builds up and causes swelling and irritation, again due to repetitive motion, such as repeated picking, plucking, and fretting motions, or extension of the thumb, such as when the left hand reaches the thumb over the top of the instrument's neck to fret or simply remain there. Signs of this problem are burning, tingling, and numbness on the thumb side of the forearm, which sometimes spreads up the forearm and can travel down the thumb and into the wrist. This is different from carpal tunnel syndrome, which is commonly considered to be the problem when this sensation is felt because people are familiar with the term, but with DeQuervain's you do not feel these sensations in other fingers of the hand as you would in true carpal tunnel syndrome. Note: this condition should not be confused with basal joint arthritis, another problem which occurs in the thumb area and which, as a different condition, will not respond to similar treatment methods used for DeQuervain's. See the condition "basal joint arthritis", also in this chapter, for a more detailed description. See "carpal tunnel syndrome" in the conditions chapter in Volume One to learn more about that condition.

Problems in this area can arise from squeezing your thumb excessively. This can be a problem for string instrumentalists when bowing if the thumb isn't bent on the bow and able to move freely. A rigid wrist is an indicator of excessive thumb pressure. Having the wrist in a neutral position as much as possible is helpful to avoid wrist injury, but this does not mean keeping the wrist rigid, as in tight and stiff and straight. Allow the thumb and wrist to relax by stretching or shaking them out on occasion to remind yourself that they are tight. A thumb that is pressing too hard causes the forearm to tighten up, and the forearm and wrist to become rigid. Releasing the thumb allows the arm and wrist to move freely. This can be tested by trying this experiment away from your instrument: move your arm as if bowing while pressing with your thumb into your forefinger. Then release your thumb and move your arm as if continuing bowing. See how your hand is now able to move freely when your thumb is relaxed.

Changing these few things as described and utilizing proper stretching and warming up will many times help significantly with DeQuervain's syndrome. If it becomes a chronic problem, returning often or not improving with simpler measures, ultrasound is a therapeutic modality which can help to reduce pain by reducing inflammation and increasing circulation, and acupuncture is also great for this and for pain relief also.

DeQuervain's Syndrome – What to do

- For purposes of prevention, one should keep their thumb slightly bent, or flexed, at all times, which is a natural position for it to take. Keeping the thumb in a straight position stresses the joints, especially when you're bearing a load, as in holding your instrument. Bassists can experience severe problems in this area as their thumbs are commonly kept in this position for hours at a time. Bassists that utilize bowing also tend to squeeze the thumb, keeping it rigid when it should bend on the bow and enjoy free motion. Again, shaking out your wrist from time to time will keep it from becoming and remaining too rigid, which along with tight forearm musculature promotes excess thumb pressure and continuation of the problem. Relaxation of these areas by shaking them out will release this excess thumb pressure, and less thumb pressure will keep these areas relaxed.

- Try this exercise away from your instrument. Move your arm in a bowing motion while pressing with your thumb into your forefinger. Release your thumb and move your arm once again as if bowing. See how your hand is able to move freely when your thumb is relaxed and not pressing into the finger, i.e. the bow. This is a much more desirable position to find oneself in than dealing with unnecessary rigidity of the thumb or the wrist.
- Avoid extreme positions of the wrist, especially when your thumb is at an angle. Your wrists should be as close to a neutral position as possible at all times. Double bassists should be especially aware when playing to not exaggerate the motions of raising and lowering of the wrist during bow strokes. If you minimize thumb pressure, as previously discussed, your hand and wrist motion will be fluid. Double bassists should avoid long periods of playing in high positions with extreme left wrist positions, and pay attention to the right hand when playing pizzicato. Double bassists should release the thumb as one reaches toward the upper positions before undertaking thumb positions, especially for those players with smaller hands who should get into thumb position sooner to avoid overstretching the thumb. One should also be mindful of squeezing the fingerboard with one's left thumb. Better to keep it relaxed to avoid injury and enable greater facility on the fingerboard.
- The thumb can be stabilized, when necessary, by splinting or taping to prevent excessive extension, to be followed after removal by light circular range of motion exercises. These exercises should not be performed too soon, or too vigorously, so as not to reaggravate or exacerbate an already existing injury.
- During practice or performance, rest your thumb as often as possible, occasionally and gently moving it in circles to keep circulation flowing. Remember when doing this to not exceed a normal, or non-painful range of motion. Take the thumb off of the instrument, and let it hang by your side. Double bassists should take the thumb off of the bow. This gives the thumb a few seconds of release, returning it afterward as closely as possible to a neutral position. One can also do this with the index finger to give it a break by lifting it off the bow from time to time. Even a few seconds of this provides relief and can keep excess tension from building up.
- The classic provocative test for DeQuervain's is an orthopedic test called Finkelstein's test, which reproduces the symptoms, i.e. pain, by the examiner either placing or asking the patient to form a fist over the thumb, and then ulnar deviating, or moving the wrist in a downward motion towards the pinky side of the hand *(See Figure 1 a & b).*
- Symptoms can be diminished by resting the area, remembering to not push or grip too tightly with the thumb, and to use good posture principles to lessen tension in general whenever possible (see the posture section in Ch. 3 of *The Bassist's Guide to Injury Management, Prevention, & Better Health - Volume One* for correct posture examples). Alternate fingerings can also be an option.
- Treatment options include the previously mentioned splinting, anti-inflammatories, ultrasound, acupuncture, and, if conservative methods fail, steroid injections or possible surgery to decompress the compartment. Recurrence of DeQuervain's, if conditions are not corrected and/or causative factors are repeated, is frequent.

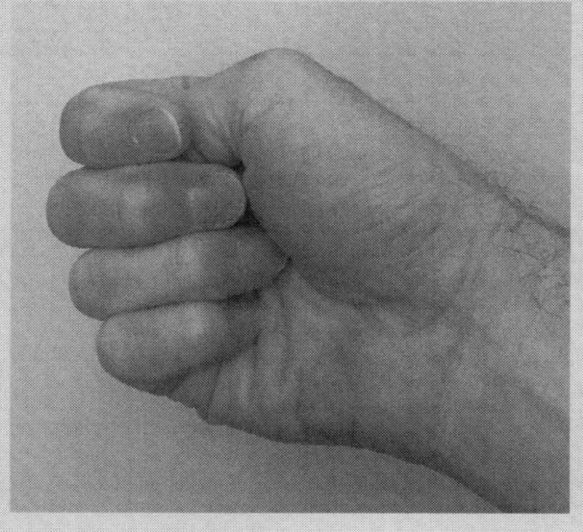

Figure 1 a) Finkelstein's Test for DeQuervain's Syndrome

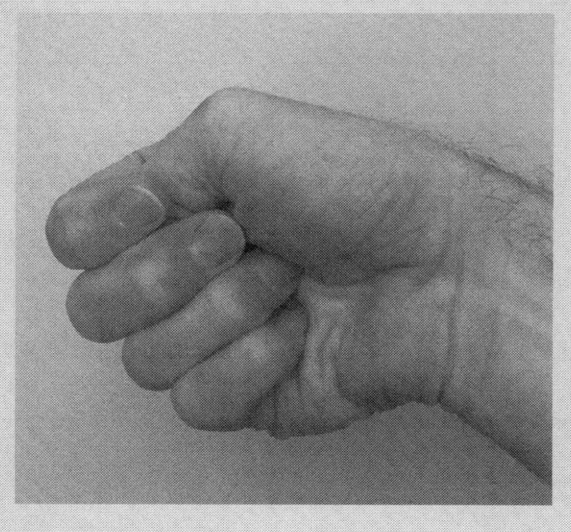

Figure 1 b) with ulnar deviation

DUPUYTREN'S CONTRACTURE

Dupuytren's contracture will present with the following symptoms:

- **a tightening and thickening in the palm of the hand, causing the fingers, usually the 4th and 5th, to curl up as a result.**

Dupuytren's Contracture – What it is

Dupuytren's contracture is usually seen in men over 50 years of age, is genetically inherited, and presents in a tough fibrous sheet of tissue called the palmar aponeurosis, which spreads across the palm of the hand from the crease area at the wrist to the bases of the fingers, and which covers the flexor tendons that are located and travel there. In this condition, this sheet of tissue thickens and tightens, causing the fingers to curl up or flex uncontrollably due to the compression of the aforementioned flexor tendons. Effectively, the fingers will bend towards the palm, and one will not be able to straighten them. It can affect one hand or both, and may not be evident in the palm but instead seen as a small nodule or bump affecting the base of the fourth or fifth fingers or both, on the palmar, or palm up, side of the hand. Most often in my experience it will be seen in the palm, and will have a puckering up or pinching type of appearance. This condition should not be confused with trigger finger, or flexor tenosynovitis, in which a finger gets stuck in a bent position and in a stuttering or snapping fashion straightens on its own or must be straightened out by the individual (see *The Bassist's Guide to Injury Management, Prevention, & Better Health - Volume One* for more details on this condition).

Dupuytren's Contracture – What to do

- Treatment for this condition almost, if not always, requires surgery to release the tendons, which often has a positive result with minimum playing time lost before one may resume their normal activities. Other methods, such as ultrasound, deep tissue massage, active release, and acupuncture are worth trying, but have been found to be ineffective in my experience.

ESSENTIAL TREMOR

Essential Tremor will present with the following symptoms:

- involuntary, rhythmic shaking.

Essential Tremor – What it is

Essential tremor is categorized as a neurological disorder which causes involuntary and rhythmic shaking, especially when one does simple tasks, such as drinking from a glass or tying one's shoelaces. While it can affect almost any part of the body, it occurs most often in the hands. It will typically worsen over time, and can become severe. It differs from Parkinson's disease, with which it is frequently mistaken, as it occurs usually when the hands are in use, while Parkinson's is most prominent when your hands are at your sides, resting in the lap, or when moving, in a motion known as "pill rolling." Parkinson's also causes other health issues, whereas essential tremor, while often progressively worsening, remains a tremor.

Essential Tremor – What to do

- While many mild cases don't require treatment, there are some pharmacological options, as well as botox injections, which can help temporarily if the condition proves to be interfering with daily activities.
- Physical therapy, designed to teach one exercises to improve muscle strength, control, and coordination, can be useful.
- Occupational therapy to help one to adapt to living with this condition can also be helpful. This can include using heavier glasses and utensils, and wearing wrist weights while playing instruments.
- Deep brain stimulation, a surgical procedure in which a probe is inserted into the thalamus (the part of the brain causing the tremors), and which then runs through a wire to a neurostimulator, or pacemaker-like device implanted in the chest in order to interrupt signals from the thalamus via electrical impulses, can be considered if tremors are severely disabling and other methods don't work, but as one can imagine this is highly invasive.
- Avoiding caffeine and other stimulants can help control tremors.
- Alcohol use, while seeming to initially help to calm tremors, can cause them to worsen once its effects wear off, and can lead to alcoholism as the body continually requires more alcohol to achieve the perceived calming result.
- Relaxation techniques such as massage and meditation can be helpful.

FOCAL DYSTONIA (MUSICIAN'S DYSTONIA, DYSTONIA)

Focal dystonia will present with the following symptoms:

- abnormal or involuntary movements of the hands and fingers including muscle cramps, spasms, and curling of the fingers, presenting in musicians only when attempting to play an instrument, and with one not being in control of these symptoms.

Focal Dystonia – What it is

A dystonia is a movement disorder in which an individual's muscles contract, or tighten, uncontrollably. Focal dystonia of the hand for the musician presents as a loss of control of the hand and fingers when playing an instrument, and, unless concurrent with another condition, not affecting other activities. Some researchers believe it to be caused by continuous rapid movements of the hands and fingers, such as in the playing of an instrument, most often through over-practice, while some feel it is miscommunication between opposing muscle groups, called agonists and antagonists, which should alternate between contracting and relaxing but in this case tighten at the same time. Some take it a step farther, and postulate that this dysfunction between the muscle groups is caused by an overload of specific mechanisms in the brain, which are designed to coordinate all the activity required by the body to allow muscles to operate efficiently. Testing to confirm this has shown through brain mapping (study of the brain's structure) that the dystonic areas (those showing dysfunction) were disorganized anatomically and functionally. These areas overlapped and lost specificity, leading to a loss of control and coordination and causing dystonia to manifest physically. Further brain imaging studies have shown that musicians with dystonia have finger representations in their brains that are abnormally fused compared to those who don't have dystonia, resulting in instructions from the brain potentially going to incorrect muscles. This would often make the performer, who usually senses these changes slowly yet substantially, practice harder, in frequency and in physical force, in an attempt to regain this sudden loss of control. As the brain can remake itself through a process called neuroplasticity which allows it to be shaped by need, use, and experience, this leads to another question, namely is the dystonia a physical process causing the brain to map the areas incorrectly and/or reshape them as previously described, or is the brain genetically predisposed to dystonia in some, most, or all cases, making this condition inevitable for some?

This condition is called focal because it is specific to a muscle or group of muscles and to an activity as previously stated. Dystonia refers to the abnormal movements and postures displayed. This condition has also been thought to be caused, partially or completely, by other provoking factors, such as anxiety, poor posture, altered biomechanics (faulty technique resulting in acquired faulty patterns when playing/practicing, which become reinforced through repetition and part of the performer's repertoire), pain (though pain is usually not present with the symptoms), and abnormal sensory input from the brain. Further causes put forth as possible triggers include a sudden increase in playing or practice time, dramatic change in technique, return to play following an extended break, trauma, a history of nerve injury, and a change of instrument (whether size, type or family). Neurologic and orthopedic tests will return normal, as the problems are, again, occurring only during playing. EMG (electromyography), which evaluates and records the electrical activity produced by muscles at rest and during contraction, may confirm the focal dystonia diagnosis. Once present, the symptoms will progressively worsen over time. Playing more, taking breaks, and taking time away from the instrument all have proven unsuccessful as stand-alone treatment methods. Noted neurologist and author Oliver Sacks describes a case study in his book Musicophilia, in which a concert violinist begins to lose control over the third finger of his left hand, quits playing for 3 months, and upon resuming playing finds the condition has spread to his 4th and 5th fingers.

Dystonia will start as small errors in a normal practice or performance routine, such as not being able to hold down a string, or missing a note in what would normally be a simple matter of technique, such as a scale or a familiar passage or motion. This will occur suddenly, without warning, and will become noticeable as it continues and worsens. Again, since it is not painful and does not affect other activity, at first it is easy to overlook.

Sometimes dystonia will present along with other conditions, the most common being ulnar neuropathy, or cubital tunnel syndrome, described in depth in *The Bassist's Guide to Injury Management, Prevention & Better Health - Volume One*. Trigger finger is another possible condition which can coexist with or can morph into dystonia, again described in detail in the previous volume of this book. Initially painless, when other factors such as muscular contractions, muscular compensation, passage of time, and the stress that comes with these issues enter into the equation, pain can become a factor. Again, rest may not help, except in situations where we are treating other conditions concurrently, in which case it may or may not be a useful adjunct to successfully treat the dystonia.

Depending on the instrument, the player, and the study, different fingers or configurations of fingers have been identified as most likely to be affected. According to the Musicians with Dystonia group, string players usually develop this in their left hands, while guitarists and percussionists can develop it in either hand. Also proposed is that the hand that performs the most complex movement patterns is usually the one that is affected, so the issue seems to be more dependent on the instrument played than on hand dominance.

Focal Dystonia – What to do

Many treatment methods have been proposed and tried in the treatment of focal dystonia, with varying degrees of success. The following are the more successful, promising, or interesting ones

- **Botox**
  Botulinum toxin type a, or botox, is a drug made from a toxin produced by the bacterium Clostridium Botulinum. This same toxin causes a life-threatening type of food poisoning called botulism. It can be used in small doses to treat health problems and cosmetic imperfections, and has been used as a treatment method for focal dystonia as well. It is injected into the affected muscles, and can provide temporary relief by weakening or paralyzing muscles or blocking nerves that supply those muscles. Temporary is the key word, as effects will typically last from 3-4 months. Side effects can include pain at the injection site, flu-like symptoms, headache, upset stomach, and trouble breathing and swallowing according to the United States Food and Drug Administration. Other downsides can include operator error, such as injection of the wrong area due to faulty diagnosis or technique, which could paralyze the area and interfere with the performer's ability to play. Botox has helped some return to performance, most notably pianist Leon Fleischer, who famously was forced to quit playing due to dystonia, only to return to playing after a combination of botox treatment and a technique called Rolfing, a type of bodywork. It should be noted that, even under the best circumstances and with the best outcome, these Botox injections will not remove the underlying neural or possible genetic problems associated with this condition, and that the treatments will need to be repeated to continue to be effective. The body also may develop a resistance after repeated injections, much as with antibiotics, rendering the treatment after a time ineffective. Injections with botulinum may also afford the player the opportunity to reassess hand and wrist positioning and technique, in this way interrupting the established physical patterns that have possibly led or contributed to this condition, and offer a "fresh start" through better coordination and biomechanics. No cases have been found by this author to suggest that true focal dystonia has been attributed strictly to a physical cause such as tight musculature and cured, meaning no return occurrences, through injection of botulinum toxin.
- **Pharmacology**
  Anticholinergic drugs and/or beta blockers are thought to be helpful by affecting transmission of messages from the brain to the muscles. This method of treatment has not proven especially successful, as these drugs are meant for use for other conditions and have considerable side effects that accompany them. The rationale for this treatment, postulating that there is in effect a disconnect between the brain and the affected musculature, this causing the dystonia, is a popular and plausible theory.
- **Retraining Exercises**
  Retraining exercises are based upon the notion that through physical (such as practicing too hard or too much) or neurological means (by recognizing faulty physical patterns as "normal" and "correct"), or via a combination of both, including any emotional stressors arising from this condition, the body has been trained to perform in a faulty way, and that it can be retrained to eliminate these faulty patterns and play in a dystonia-free fashion. Sometimes these exercises work, and sometimes not. They may be utilized in conjunction with some of the other discussed treatment methods, or not. There is no single protocol which, if followed to the letter, will always yield a positive result.

Most of these exercises involve taking the problem area, which could be the particular piece of music, the motion, or the hand itself, and identifying the point of breakdown, or when the dystonia occurs. The idea is that the dystonia should not occur if one stays below a certain application or threshold of force for a period of time sufficient for the body (including the brain/central nervous system) to recognize, accept, and make appropriate adjustments, or to simply carry out its inherent "normal" dystonia free function unimpeded, in this way creating a new pattern. Factors involved appear to include time spent playing, force used while playing, motion involved, speed of motion and force, and overall stress levels, physical and mental, including muscle tightness. Filming oneself during these sessions can help to identify the points at which there is or is not a dystonia occurring, and in this way can provide a baseline reference and serve as positive reinforcement as progress is made.

One patient I have worked with, an electric bassist, has focal dystonia, diagnosed by my office. He plays mostly 5 and 6 string basses. He has dystonia in the fourth and fifth fingers of his left (fretting) hand, which usually "don't work" when playing. After ruling out other causes, I gave him a series of specific finger exercises to perform, incorporating different configurations of one finger per fret patterns from top to bottom of the neck, on all strings, asking him to do these daily and to do them on a four string bass to start with in order to change things up and rule out the possibility of simple hand and wrist fatigue type issues. These included isolating fingers by performing the same motions two fingers at a time, for example index-middle, then middle-ring, followed by ring-pinky, then index-ring, followed by middle-pinky. The patient was to report back to me any problems or improvements noticed. The patient was instructed to use a metronome at first, to set a tempo so that we knew how fast or slow he was going and we could adjust it from there as necessary. He was not to use the metronome throughout the exercises, although this could have been incorporated later if results were not impressive without its use. After a period of doing this, we added finger weights to the equation, a product which slipped onto and added small amounts of weight to each finger, the idea being when you took them off your fingers would "fly across the fingerboard." In this case, we wanted to assess if the extra weight and the slowing down it naturally produced would make a difference in playing and in the presence or level of the dystonia. I also asked the patient to experiment with different left hand positions, such as keeping the thumb squarely in the middle of the neck, bringing the thumb up over the top of the neck, or moving it and the wrist as the fingers went up and down from the E to G strings in a continuously rotating fashion. All of the above methods were added in layers, in the order listed, to differentiate what was and was not working and from there adjusted accordingly.

As of this writing the patient has reported some improvements, and is able to play his instrument with intermittent bouts of dystonia, however he has not experienced a complete eradication of symptoms.

In another example, guitarist Billy McLaughlin, after being afflicted with focal dystonia, has gone on to switch dominant hands, from playing right-handed to left, and has enjoyed a successful career by doing this. Others have not been so fortunate, switching dominant hands and having the same problem then occur on the opposite side.

- **Splinting/Immobilization**
Splinting or immobilization of the dystonic unit or area has been tried with the thought that it would, by prevention of movement of the area, reduce the possibility of the brain sensing that the fingers are overlapping in its cortical map, causing anatomical and functional disorganization and a loss of specificity, i.e. the dystonia. The downside to this is that the muscle atrophy, or disuse that will occur from the treatment, will necessitate strengthening exercises to restore normal strength and motion, which could prove problematic.

In another notable instance, splints were used to immobilize one or more digits other than the dystonic finger. The musicians were then instructed to perform repetitive exercises with the dystonic finger along with one or more of the non-splinted fingers for a period of eight days. The results of this were that the side of the body treated became more like the unaffected side, and improvement had taken place.

- To help avoid focal dystonia, as always pay attention to technique and follow healthy habits as outlined in this book. When making changes in playing, such as technique, wrist angle etc., try playing new things. Old habits reinforce old patterns, and through muscle memory (brain patterns telling the body what to do) this can mean the difference between real change and reinforcement of the old, sometimes to one's detriment.

- **Change things up**
  As we are dealing with a faulty brain map as previously described, anyone dealing with dystonia is trying to establish new patterns and break the old problematic ones. This may be by stimulating growth of new neurons (which would create a new map), by forming an additional map, or by altering the old map to accommodate the new pattern. Due to the individuality of each case, there is unfortunately no one right way to fix this problem.

  Additional ways to try to deal with this issue include practicing with a blindfold, watching oneself practice slowly one finger at a time with a mirror to establish when and at what point dystonia begins, taping oneself in performance/practice to establish when and at what point dystonia begins, and raising or lowering the action on the instrument and/or other adjustments designed to distract the brain from falling into faulty patterns. It has been found that symptoms can be lessened through sensory tricks such as playing instruments wearing a latex or other textural glove, thereby altering the sensory input received by the brain. Another suggestion is to do exercises, such as the retraining exercises mentioned previously, but with an external source to distract, such as while watching television to take the brain's focus off of the problem.

  In all cases, it is vital to correctly diagnose the problem as a dystonia, and not simply a musculoskeletal disorder or a dystonia in conjunction with a musculoskeletal disorder, which should be treated as such. With a proper diagnosis, a strategy can be developed and one can be taught to incorporate proper postural and technique considerations to assist in treatment and to help prevent recurrence.

  It is safe to say that in the present day there is no definitive treatment method for focal dystonia. Something that the author is excited about is the work of VS Ramachandran, who has used what he calls a mirror box method to elicit motion in phantom limbs. Phantom limbs are limbs that through amputation are missing but still have a cortical representation, meaning there is still a memory of these limbs in the brain, making one able to feel sensation in an arm or leg even though no physical manifestation exists. In this extraordinary phenomenon, one can point to a feeling of pain or itching or a similar sensation in space where it would be found on a limb under normal circumstances. Through his mirror box method, Ramachandran shows the patient a mirror image of their intact limb, and has them move the limb. The mirror image of the intact limb is seen by the eye in the place of the missing limb, and in this way the missing limb is registered by the brain as being present. The patient's sensation in the non-existent limb is by this method recognized as present and legitimate by the brain, and the bodily sensation can be addressed and resolved. Ramachandran suggests this method can be extrapolated to other conditions, such as stroke, or focal dystonia.

FROZEN SHOULDER

Frozen shoulder, or *adhesive capsulitis*, will usually present with some or all of the following symptoms:

- **pain in the shoulder, generated from the supraspinatus tendon *(see figure 2)* resulting in an inability to lift the arm out to the side, like a wing, or a general inability to move the arm/shoulder without great pain.**

Frozen Shoulder or Adhesive Capsulitis – What it is

Frozen shoulder, or adhesive capsulitis, is characterized by significant loss of range of motion and a sensation of deep pain, and is most commonly caused by trauma, overuse, or can present post surgically in the shoulder area, usually the rotator cuff. Symptoms usually begin with pain in the shoulder in the area of the supraspinatus tendon, with a steady decrease in range of motion due to inability to raise the arm in abduction (sideways away from the body) due to pain. If one has had rotator cuff surgery and hasn't followed up adequately or properly with their physical therapy, frozen shoulder can often result due to a build-up of scar tissue and reduced range of motion.

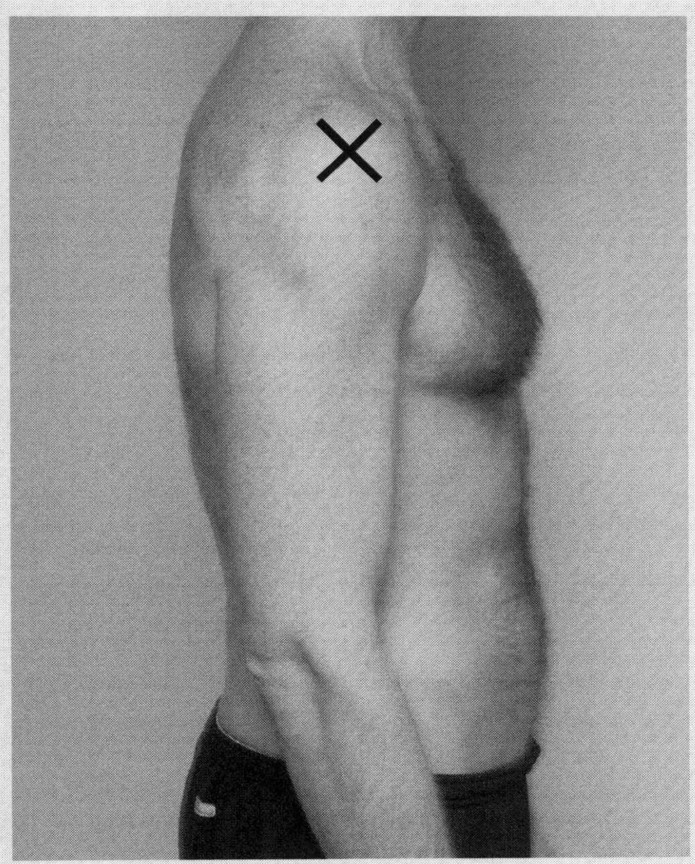

Figure 2. Supraspinatus tendon location on the shoulder.

Frozen Shoulder or Adhesive Capsulitis – What to do

Frozen shoulder needs to be treated as soon as possible to avoid potential loss of partial or full range of motion.

- acupuncture can help with pain relief and to break up adhesions.
- interferential current can help with pain relief and to break up adhesions.
- stretching and active and passive range of motion exercises are necessary to break up adhesions.
- cross friction massage (a specialized type of massage to break up scar tissue) at and around the supraspinatus tendon can help break up adhesions from frozen shoulder. This is best followed by range of motion exercises, specifically abduction, which is best done by a health care professional with experience in this area. This can be a game of degrees, a few at a time, and can take anywhere from several weeks minimum to several months maximum to regain full range of motion. The shoulder may never reach its maximum range of motion, depending on the severity of the injury causing the problem, and how much time has elapsed between when the injury occurred and when treatment began.
- ultrasound on the area of the supraspinatus tendon will help to reduce inflammation of the bursa and promote further relaxation of the area, and is usually most effective after stretching, exercise, or massage of the area has been performed.

More common shoulder problems for the bassist are described in *The Bassist's Guide to Injury Management, Prevention & Better Health - Volume One.*

TMJ (TEMPOROMANDIBULAR JOINT DYSFUNCTION), CMD (CRANIOMANDIBULAR DYSFUNCTION)

TMJ will present with some or all of the following symptoms:

- pain in the jaw and/or side of the face, at rest or while chewing
- clicking or popping of the jaw when opening or closing the mouth
- accompanying symptoms which can include headaches, neck pain and/or stiffness, locked jaw, ear pain, and ringing in the ears

TMJ – What it is

TMJ, or temporomandibular dysfunction, refers to the areas in the face and jaw that are affected, while craniomandibular dysfunction refers to pain which is predominant in the head, neck and jaw areas.

CMD in musicians most frequently presents as pain in the shoulder and/or upper extremity, followed by neck pain, then pain in the teeth/TMJ (temporomandibular joint) regions.

The most common joint affected by this disorder, the TMJ (temporomandibular joint), connects the mandible, or lower part of the jawbone, to the skull at the temporal bone, which lies in front of the ear. In between these bones is a tiny disc of cartilage, which can become displaced for several reasons, commonly through tightness of associated musculature. Causes for this are numerous, however this joint is responsible for jaw movement, including chewing, swallowing, breathing and talking, so it's not difficult to see how this can easily occur in non-musical as well as performance settings. Symptoms, besides pain, can be felt at rest or while chewing, and include clicking or popping of the jaw, often felt as if the jaw were coming out of place, headaches or facial pain, neck pain and/or stiffness, locked jaw, ear pain, and ringing of the ears.

TMJ – What to do

Treatment for this disorder begins with a proper diagnosis. If the patient has pain, one would first look for tight musculature in the surrounding area and try to reduce this through various therapy techniques, some of which are:

- massage and trigger point therapy which can help to loosen up tight musculature that is pulling on the affected structures, keeping them tight and causing pain.
- ultrasound; some practitioners maintain ultrasound helps reduce inflammation and reduce pain, while some feel this area is too close to the brain and that ultrasound may cause damage there and/or to associated structures. Exercise caution: the author personally feels that there could be risk in using ultrasound for this condition due to its deep and penetrating nature, and does not utilize it in treatment.
- acupuncture can be very useful in the treatment of TMJ by relaxing musculature and reducing inflammation.
- chiropractic adjustments can reset the proper alignment of the jaw if it is misaligned, usually noted by popping or clicking of the jaw when opening and/or closing the mouth.
- posture and awareness are very important in prevention of temporomandibular joint and craniomandibular dysfunction. This includes relaxing the appropriate muscle groups. Learn the anatomy. Take a breath, focus on these muscles and relax them one at a time through focus and breathing. By doing this before beginning to play and thus establishing a learned pattern, one can dramatically reduce the likelihood of an incident occurring. Don't set or clench the jaw before playing due to tension, nervousness, or habit. Grinding one's teeth at night can also be a factor. In this case, a night guard, or occlusal splint may be prescribed to keep this from happening.

WRIST, HAND, FINGER PROBLEMS

Wrist, hand, and finger problems can be numerous, and have been described under their specific conditions elsewhere in this chapter and in The Bassist's Guide to Injury Management, Prevention & Better Health - Volume One. Here are some conditions that don't fall into any of the previously covered categories:

- **All fingers curling up, with pain and difficulty moving, randomly occurring (not happening at any specific time, or in relation to playing an instrument), not related to any injury, or to any increase in playing, practice time, or any other overuse.**

  While there could be several causes for a condition of this type, if arthritis and repetitive stress type injuries have been ruled out, imaging or other testing has ruled out more serious pathology, and another logical diagnosis cannot be reached, one should consider personal habits. Sleeping position is important, in that if one sleeps on their stomach, they can experience neck stiffness from sleeping in the same position for several hours at a time, causing muscles in the neck, back, and shoulders to tighten and stay tight rather than get the relaxation that rest brings. Also, when one sleeps with their arm stretched out overhead, or underneath their body in a cramped position, this can cause numbness in the arm which may radiate into the extremity by pinching nerves that can last into the following day or longer if this position is repeated often enough. This can apply to the hands themselves, as even if our sleeping position is correct, by sleeping on our sides, if one keeps the wrists bent and hands balled up under the head or pillow, this can lead to pain there that can be eradicated by simply being aware of the problem and not curling up the hands. Understanding that one is not aware of their hand and body positioning when they are sleeping, if one starts out properly, this will be learned by the body as proper behavior and be less likely to go to a problematic position later. Sometimes, especially after the age of 30, glucosamine can help to hydrate joints in the hand and help with random aches and soreness there, but its use should be discussed with a health care professional.

- **Numbness in fourth and fifth fingers.**

  At one point, I had several patients come to me within a few month period with numbness in their little and ring fingers. They all said that it had been there for a long period of time, had no obvious cause, and that it would sometimes come and go but always return. There was no increase in symptoms when playing their instruments. The sensation mostly seemed to be coming from the elbow, and even though all the players were right-handed, the sensation didn't always affect the same side in each player. After treating the players for golfer's elbow (medial epicondylitis), ulnar tunnel syndrome, and watching them play to identify bad habits that could cause or contribute to their symptoms, I was mostly successful in alleviating their symptoms but in some the problem returned shortly thereafter. Sometimes with symptoms like this surgery is necessary, in which the nerve is relocated from the groove next to the elbow to the front of the elbow, thus freeing a nerve that could easily become entrapped and a chronic condition depending on the nature of the repetitious activity. While this is usually a successful and low risk type of procedure, one still wants to avoid surgery whenever possible. Flying to a lecture a couple of months later, I noticed that I had some numbness in my fourth and fifth fingers, which is not normal for me. I shook my hands and arms out and resumed my reclining position, only to have the sensation return several minutes later. Looking down, I noticed that my arm was lying on the arm rest, and the side of the rest was digging into the area where the ulnar nerve was located at the elbow, causing direct pressure on the nerve and resulting in numbness and tingling in those same fingers. Many times, when sitting in a chair with a side arm rest, or in our cars with a side rest or console, our arms will lie in such a way that it is comfortable to lay the elbow, and in this way the groove where the ulnar nerve sits, right on the side of the arm rest or console, the result of which is this numbness and tingling in the fourth and fifth fingers *(see figure 3)*. Being aware of this in our everyday non-playing lives enables us to keep the arms at our side, in our laps, or in another position so that this doesn't happen. Another symptom that can occur from this can be a 'trigger finger' effect in the fifth or pinky finger, in which the finger fails to open completely at times, stuttering as it tries to straighten. While this can be symptomatic of trigger finger as described earlier in the chapter, it can also be due to this same detrimental arm position or sleeping with the hands curled up as described in the previous condition.

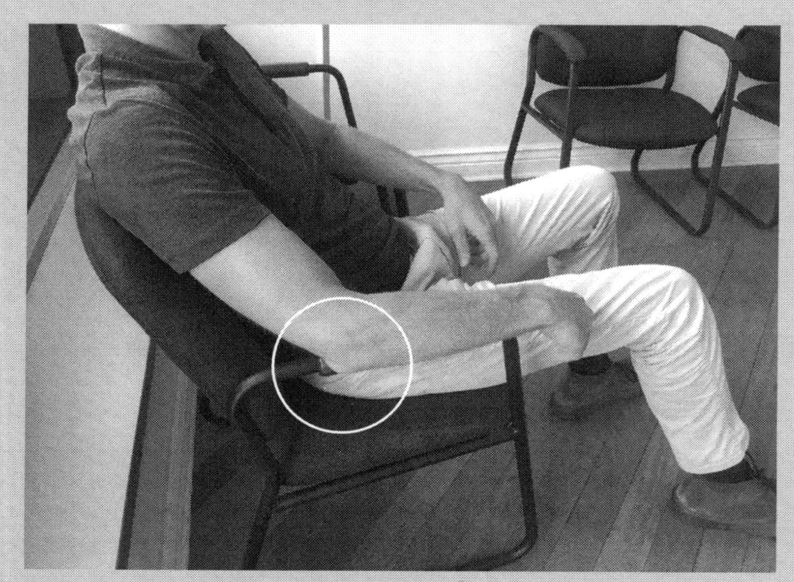

Figure 3. Compression of the ulnar nerve against the arm of a chair.

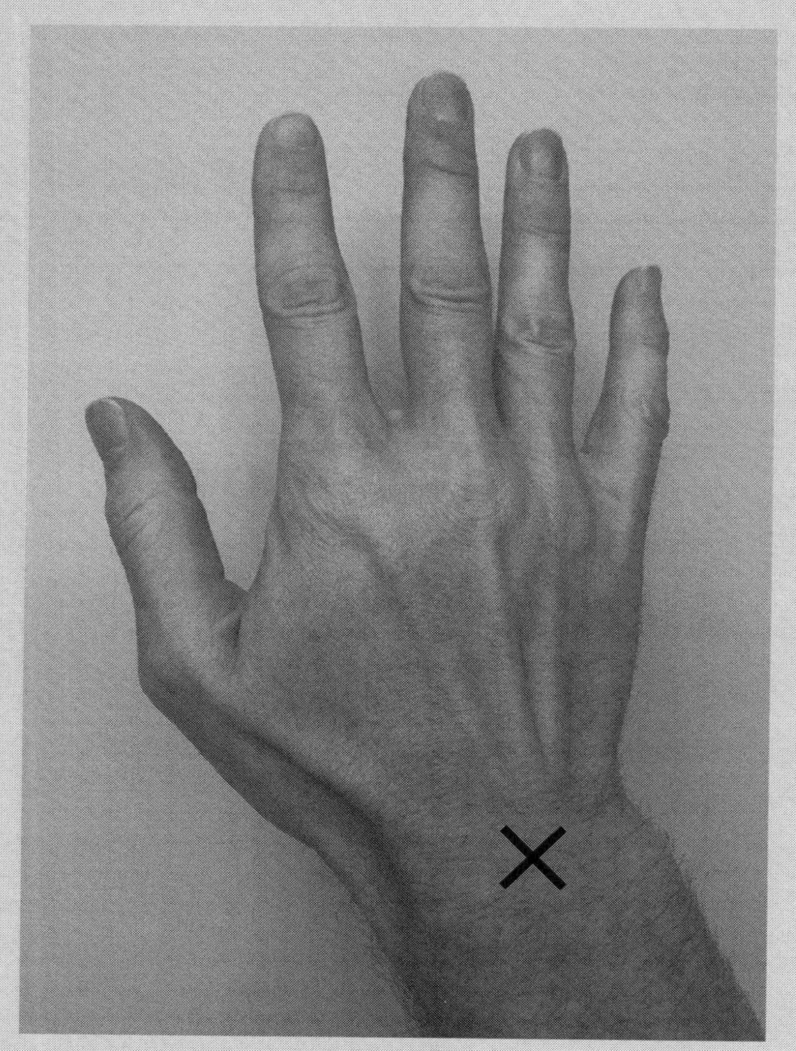

Figure 4. Location of the lunate, a frequently restricted carpal bone and site of pain in the bassist.

- **Pain on the back of the hand, usually at the wrist and just above (towards the fingers but not going into the fingers).**

Many musicians, especially electric bassists, have come to me with pain in the back of the hand at the wrist. It presents as local (stays in one area), and is present only on the back of the hand and not the palm side. It does not radiate pain, numbness or tingling into the fingers or up the arm. Palpation reveals a restriction of the carpal bones of the hand in general, and of the lunate bone in particular *(see figure 4)*. This condition can be called a restriction, or subluxation, of the carpal bones, which means less than a dislocation.

The most common restriction or subluxation in the wrist that I see for all musicians, particularly bassists, and for many non-musicians is of the previously mentioned lunate bone. The shape of this bone and its position in the back of the hand makes it particularly prone to restriction. Forceful compression of the lunate by flexion of the wrist, as in many instrument playing positions, pushes this bone forward against surrounding bones and structures, causing its restriction or subluxation and many times that of the other carpal bones around it. This condition may come and go spontaneously depending on how long this has been going on and how far it has progressed. It can arise in either hand, but more frequently in the right hand in right handed players who use a finger style technique, which utilizes constant repetitive motion of the fingers. Often this will be seen there when one increases their playing time, doesn't take frequent breaks, digs in more aggressively, or comes back to playing after a long break away from the instrument.

Occasionally a problem in this area will be accompanied by neurologic symptoms if the subluxated lunate presses on the carpal tunnel, which will then present with symptoms as previously described in the condition carpal tunnel syndrome in *The Bassist's Guide to Injury Management, Prevention, & Better Health - Volume One*. Treatment of these cases in the case of a restriction/subluxation is often very successful, with manipulation being the most effective way to restore motion, which is often immediate. Depending on the level of tension in the muscles of the forearm which pull on the tendons that attach to the bones in the hand and wrist area, this condition may recur frequently until this tension is addressed. Most musicians with this issue will resume their normal workload and musical career after successful treatment, with this condition then many times becoming an occasional annoyance, returning due to the repetitive motions that playing places these structures under. The best way I find to administer these manipulations is with a device called a toggle board, which one can ask their health care practitioner if they have available. Manipulation without this device, in which the practitioner takes the wrist and applies a jerking, whip-like motion can be successful, but also carries with it a degree of non-specificity due to its lack of complete control, and can cause damage to the surrounding structures if not performed carefully and precisely, which this motion is not known for. For more serious cases such as a dislocation, manipulation under anesthesia can be performed. Once again, it is important to diagnose and treat this condition as soon as possible, as the longer the lunate remains restricted, subluxated, or dislocated the greater the likelihood of circulatory changes and of the surrounding structures involved remaining deformed and problematic. Kienbock's disease is a condition affecting the lunate in which blood supply to the bone is interrupted, leading to bone death, or osteo or avascular necrosis. The cause of this condition is unknown, but should be diagnosed properly as soon as possible through imaging such as x-ray, CT scan, or MRI.

There are many techniques for healing, and in this chapter and in *The Bassist's Guide to Injury Management, Prevention, & Better Health - Volume One*, we have touched on some of the more common and effective ones. It is important to have an open mind when trying unfamiliar treatment options, for many times recovery depends on what the mind believes and is willing to accept. For the individual, one technique may resonate over others, and this can make the difference between healing and not. Conversely, if something isn't working or if there is pain involved in the treatment, one should relay their concerns to their health care practitioner without delay to see if changes should be made.

CHAPTER THREE

Technique - The Way You Play

Technique is a very personal thing, and like a lot of things, there are a few "right", or accepted ways to do something and a lot of variations thereof. Sometimes variations are necessary, and many times are directly related to physical issues, such as the size of one's hands or body structure. The "technique" that I will refer to is based on the most commonly accepted style(s) that one would be exposed to by a teacher, method book, or instructional program related to the instrument, to then be adapted to the player as necessary. In other words, I'm not trying to teach, advance, or particularly change anyone's technique, but make suggestions that one can utilize with already established principles or playing style in order to give one the best chances to be and remain injury-free.

The key to this, I feel, is through awareness of possible trouble areas a player may face, and by knowing them one can avoid them as much as possible.

As such, I've developed a system to develop awareness as well as technique by breaking down one's approach to the instrument in 5 points, using the acronym TIGER. TIGER is:

THOUGHT

INTENTION

GET INTO POSITION

ENGAGE

RELEASE

Let's break those down one by one:

Thought - this is simply leaving all the rest of the stuff behind and focusing the mind on what is at hand, in the present moment. This isn't the time to think about how good you are, or aren't, or the rent is due, or tomorrow you have to get up early. It's about the task at hand. You are responsible for your thoughts and actions in the present, so clear your mind, as what has happened in the past and what will happen in the future aren't relevant at this moment in time.

Intention - now that you are in the present, what are you going to do with it? How you played yesterday is not important. How you will play now is. Make it good. Having intention helps one avoid engaging old neural patterns which have guided behavior in the past and which guide your behavior now, replacing them with new patterns based on your positive intentions in the present, which in turn shape the future.

Get into position - now is the time to prepare for physical play. Before placing the hands on the instrument, take a deep breath in, lift your shoulders up to your ears, and let your shoulders drop down while exhaling through the mouth. This will loosen up the shoulders and you can start from a place of relaxation rather than tension in the neck and shoulders, which is where most of us keep excessive tension. Shake out the hands at the wrists loosely. Place your hands on the instrument in a ready to play position.

Engage - Play. Shake out hands as necessary if you feel excess tension accumulating.

Release - Just like you started, finish. Adrenaline is flowing, take a deep breath, raise the shoulders, lower the shoulders, let the breath out through the mouth. Shake out the hands. Take off or put down the instrument, and let it go.

When learned and made an established part of your routine, TIGER should take less than 30 seconds.

Double Bass Technique

Following our earlier definition of technique, I have broken down into categories things I feel are important for a double bassist to consider from an injury prevention perspective. The categories are Posture, Standing Position, Sitting Position, Prevention from a Postural Perspective, Left Hand/Side/Shoulder, Prevention from Left Hand/Side/Shoulder Perspective, Right Hand/Side/Shoulder, Prevention from Right Hand/Side/Shoulder Perspective. These categories represent a very basic overview, and further information on the conditions described and concepts covered are explored in greater detail elsewhere in this book and in *The Bassist's Guide to Injury Management, Prevention, & Better Health - Volume One.*

First, posture:

Posture

The reality of playing the double bass is that one will have to find their own way, in both standing and sitting positions, to see what suits them as they find their style. The size of the instrument demands this, and here we will present suggestions and ideas from an injury prevention perspective which will give one a foundation on which to build and then incorporate into their postures as needed.

Gary Peacock has described his approach to the double bass in daily practice as greeting and positioning himself with the instrument, and paying attention to factors such as his posture, breathing and the texture and feeling of the instrument. This may sound esoteric but really makes good sense. By taking a moment before playing, and by focusing, one becomes aware of their oneness with the instrument, and this improves the experience from an injury prevention as well as a musical perspective. A patient of mine who took lessons from Mr. Peacock in 1964 states that part of his approach included instruction on holding the bass, that the left arm should be able to sweep the whole fingerboard independently "with no hang-ups", a fluid motion, completely free, and in this way one would be able to get around the bass from top to bottom instantly without holding the bass with the left arm.

What seems clear is that despite our best efforts, the double bass will ultimately present clear challenges to our anatomy, physiology, and music making, and so a strategy must be undertaken to combat these challenges, optimally before they happen or at least before they become serious problems.

Figure 5. Leaning to one side when playing can lead to long term problems throughout the back. If the body leaning to the right appears subtle, look at the placement of the left foot at the endpin to better appreciate it, and try this posture for yourself to really understand the feeling of this position.

Standing Position

Standing position varies for the double bassist, and there are certain adjustments that can be made to compensate for less than optimal positioning from an injury prevention perspective.

Posture is obviously very important to the double bassist. The most critical time to set your posture for the double bass is when you approach the instrument. Pick it up, set up as you normally would and before playing notice how you are standing. Are you balancing your weight and the weight of the instrument together and leaning to one side? The way you start is the way you finish, and our bodies become accustomed to hours and ultimately years of this seemingly comfortable position. When you lean on one side, this makes that side of the body support more weight, yours and that of the instrument *(see figure 5)*. This will make the muscles of the back tighten up, and after remaining that way for long periods of time this becomes a learned behavior for the body, and will affect the bassist both while playing and in everyday life activities. Effectively this means that your body thinks it now should be like this, this is the new normal, and it will settle in accordingly, which will cause further imbalance as other muscle groups are affected, such as the middle back, upper back, and neck, as these muscles all interact with each other to allow the body to work efficiently. This is one of the reasons why your shoulder blades feel tight so often, whether while playing or frequently after. It is not only your arm and shoulder motion working these muscles that increases tension and can cause tightness there, but the way your body has set and been retrained according to the demands imposed upon it.

After picking up the instrument and standing as you would normally stand, now is a good time to assess posture by making sure both feet are planted firmly on the ground and that your weight is distributed evenly on both sides. When you set your bass against your body, if you can keep this even weight balance between both sides while playing this is best, whether standing in a stationary position or regularly shifting back and forth, but for those who are used to playing a certain way and won't/can't change, we can deal with this as well. It is key to remember this even weight balance, so that when you aren't playing, such as during a break in the performance when you may be waiting for someone else to solo or play their parts and you have a few moments or minutes without playing, instead of hanging over the bass or settling back even more on one side while you are resting, instead go back to that even balance point between both sides and hang out there. Hold the bass away from your body a bit if this helps. Doing this will help the muscles to relax while in a more neutral posture, and keep the body from settling into a detrimental position.

The upper back, neck and shoulders are constantly being put into compromising positions, from factors such as reading off of a music stand, bopping your head/body in time to the music, turning your head too far one way or the other, looking at the neck, exaggerated and repetitive motions by the right and left sides, and many other considerations. Aside from technique, one can refer back to an optimal posture strategy brought up previously in *The Bassist's Guide to Injury Management, Prevention & Better Health - Volume One*, in which we pretend we have a string attached to the very top of our heads going up to the sky, and let that string pull us up by the top of our heads thereby straightening out the rest of our body along with it. This keeps the spine in an upright position and allows one's shoulders to drop back and relax, as when the head is pulled up in this way the shoulders will fall back naturally. Next, take a deep breath in and let it out completely, consciously dropping your shoulders on the exhale to ensure that relaxation will happen, while keeping your head held erect by your imaginary string. You will likely feel your shoulders drop a couple or few inches. This is because most if not all of the time we are walking around with our shoulders hiked up towards our ears, creating extra tension in the neck and shoulder blades and their associated muscles. Think about this several times a day, taking a deep breath in and letting it out while dropping the shoulders, and see how much better they feel. The goal is to try and get you to think about what good posture is and what it should be. If you can't or won't alter your posture out of concern for your technique, we want to give you a place to go, a reference point for when you aren't actually applying any technique, in the form of evenly balanced weight and relaxed musculature, which can be applied when playing or any time at all. Of course, one will be leaning over the instrument and away from the instrument and bending forward to play in thumb position and all the rest of it, but with this concept of a neutral place to go to established, one can avoid chronic problems that could occur from constant postural missteps.

What many consider to be a traditional stance calls for the player to stand with the nut at about eye level, with the upper bout against the abdomen and the lower bout touching the knee. This provides relative stability and balance, and allows free access to the positions where most repertoire is played. In this position, one will have to flex the left wrist to an uncomfortable extent to play on the e string, however, and will have to adjust their wrist accordingly and briefly as necessary. When deciding one's stance with the instrument, having the nut at eye level as a default or reference position is not necessarily the best or only strategy, as we have seen that many factors go into the stance which won't all correlate with this singular factor to create the balance with the instrument that one desires.

When assessing one's standing posture, the feet must be considered as an area of possible concern. One's stance starts at ground level and works its way up, as do tensions that can and will arise from a less than optimal posture. It is advantageous to include the instrument in establishing this posture, and one should have it at the ready when setting themselves in position before playing. The first consideration in establishing a standing posture is to bring the instrument to the body, rather than the other way around. If we go to the instrument, trying to accommodate it, this will put the player at a disadvantage from the beginning. Next, one should consider the feet, and establish a balance between them and between all parts of the feet. The feet will communicate any extra tension or lack of tension we place on them to the bones, ligaments (structures which connect bone to bone), tendons (structures which connect muscles to bones), nerves, and muscles which make up the lower extremity and which connect to, thereby affecting, the trunk and all of the structures and soft tissues there, as well as those leading to the upper extremity. Therefore, any imbalance or irregularity in the feet by extension can affect any part of the body, starting from the ground up. One should consider this when selecting footwear, which should be comfortable and provide support to all parts of the feet, particularly the arches.

As we have established, body weight should be as evenly distributed as possible, if not only for balance but so that it can be shifted as needed to aid the right or left hand. If the weight of the body is all on the right side (bow side), the left hand will not have the necessary power to perform properly, and vice versa.

The corner between the side and the back of the bass should ideally be leaned against the abdomen in such a way that the instrument can balance itself without the aid of the left hand. Many players tend to place most of their weight on the right leg immediately upon starting to play, which affects the right hip by creating excess tension, this potentially causing bursitis there and over time can lead to long term injury *(see figure 5.)* This even distribution of weight concept applies to either the standing or sitting position. One may also need to adjust their endpin height once they have established their standing posture, as this can also affect the body's alignment. It is best to set the body first, and then adjust the bass height, via the endpin and any other considerations, accordingly. A bent endpin is one alternative to traditional bass stance(s), and has been used by many performers in various incarnations since its introduction. This option, by holding the instrument upright, affords the player the luxury of negotiating the instrument without feeling the weight of the instrument on the left hand, and gives one the ability to keep the right arm close to the body, as opposed to more traditional stances.

Bowing presents its own challenges to the standing position, as the player will often have to lean to the right in order to allow the bow arm to reach around the side of the instrument to access the strings, unless they rotate the instrument to the right. If one keeps the side of the bass against their stomach rather than balancing the corner of the bass there, bowing on the lower strings is impossible without moving the instrument or body to accommodate the bow. Height of the player is also a consideration, as a shorter player has to hold the left arm higher and more to the side to reach the full range, i.e. top of the fingerboard, which can cause problems with the shoulder such as tendinitis or rotator cuff issues.

In thumb position, the shoulder will support the bass as one leans forward, or as the bass leans backward. As one navigates the fingerboard, whether with the bowing arm or the left arm, some fluidity of movement with the body will be required as one leaves the security of the neutral/established position they began with to accommodate the music and the instrument. The trick is to get where you need to when you need to, and then return to the more neutral posture that you started with as soon as possible, in order to avoid development of bad habits which could lead to injury in the short or long term.

The correct height for bowing can be found by extending your arm without locking the elbow and placing it comfortably between the end of the fingerboard and the bridge. If you have to drop your shoulders to put the bow in this position, the bass is not high enough. If the bow seems to be set properly, make sure the left hand doesn't have to reach too far for first position, which would indicate the instrument is too large. One should play on the same size instrument at home and at practice or performance, as well as playing the same way, i.e. standing or sitting, as much as possible to allow the body to get used to and comfortable with its relationship with the instrument.

Many times, with the head moving in time with the music or leaning forward in order to read charts and/or to look at the neck while playing, upright players will be more prone to have stiffness and tightness in neck musculature which can cause problems ranging from soreness to pinched nerves. One solution is to get your own music stand and keep it at the proper height and placement for one's stature and current state of their eyesight.

Standing posture, as well as seated, which is covered in the next section, is vitally important in maintaining an injury free existence for the bassist. When posture is off, muscles become overutilized and transfer stress created from this overuse to other muscle groups, causing these other muscles groups to then work harder, compensating for the initial overuse and compounding the issue. A certain tension will always be present, but too much is not a good thing. When overusing certain muscles in service to the music, to play a passage, to play a note, to go to a position that is necessary, this is not to be avoided or resisted if it is appropriate, but only for the time needed to perform this particular necessity, after which one should return to a more suitable, usually neutral, posture/position as soon as one is able. If one keeps in mind the basic principles of stance and is mindful to return to that place as soon as the necessary deviation has been executed, this will be of immeasurable use from an injury prevention standpoint. Good posture will to a large degree keep the bones of the spine and skeleton in proper alignment and utilizing their proper range of motion, thus reducing restrictions in the joints, lessening muscular tension where the muscles attach to these bones, and allowing for efficient work and performance with less likelihood of injury due to overuse and/or fatigue.

Sitting Position

As has been discussed, players select and adopt a playing position that works best for them. Factors going into this decision can include musician height, hand size, and size of the instrument relative to themselves. Sitting presents at least as many challenges as standing from an injury prevention perspective, due not only to the size of the instrument, but many times from the beginning player developing and adopting a playing position that works best for them at the time and not adapting it as time passes and the player's size, stature, style and other factors may change.

Many bassists will sit on the edge of a chair or stool. This can frequently activate a muscle called the piriformis muscle and cause sciatica, which presents as pain, numbness or tingling going down the leg, starting in the buttock *(see figure 6)*. Sitting in this position should be avoided, by simply sitting further back on the seat of the stool, or adjusting the stool height accordingly. Remember to bring the instrument to you when your posture is set rather than you going to it.

Always make sure that everything is out of your back pockets when seated so that your pelvis will sit and balance evenly. An added cushion can reduce compression of the sciatic nerve. Sitting on a high stool will provide a stable foundation for the bass, but can be conducive to bad posture, as the player will often adopt a posture which will involve leaning over the bass, and often the player will, without consciously thinking about it, find that posture easier and/or more comfortable overall and remain that way. This will lead to the detrimental aspects of this position on the neck and shoulder musculature and will easily become habit if the player is not mindful of this posture and process. When in a seated position, both feet flat on the floor will reduce pressure on the low back by keeping the spine straight with the buttocks evenly balanced on the seat or edge of the stool, but again try to avoid sitting on the very edge.

Figure 6. Sitting on the edge of a stool puts pressure on the piriformis muscle, which can cause pain in the buttocks, low back, and possibly sciatica.

Once more, keep in mind that one must be careful to avoid bending over the bass too much in the neck and shoulder area, and to be mindful to return to a straight spine based posture when it is not necessary to bend over in service to the music.

When children start to play in a seated position, they will many times end up on seats which are too high, and their feet will hang down and try to find a place to rest anywhere they can. This will cause the pelvis and the low back to curve, which the body will adapt to as it becomes habit, causing tight musculature and these changes which have occurred to become problems of a more permanent nature. Another common approach to sitting for players of all ages is to sit on a stool with the left knee bent and the left foot resting on a rung of the stool, with the right leg hanging down and the right foot on the floor (or the same position with the sides switched, right knee bent and the left leg hanging down) *(see figure 7)*. While this may seem a natural position, this causes the spine to twist, which will cause discomfort in the short run and postural problems in the long run as the torso and pelvis shift to compensate for this twist.

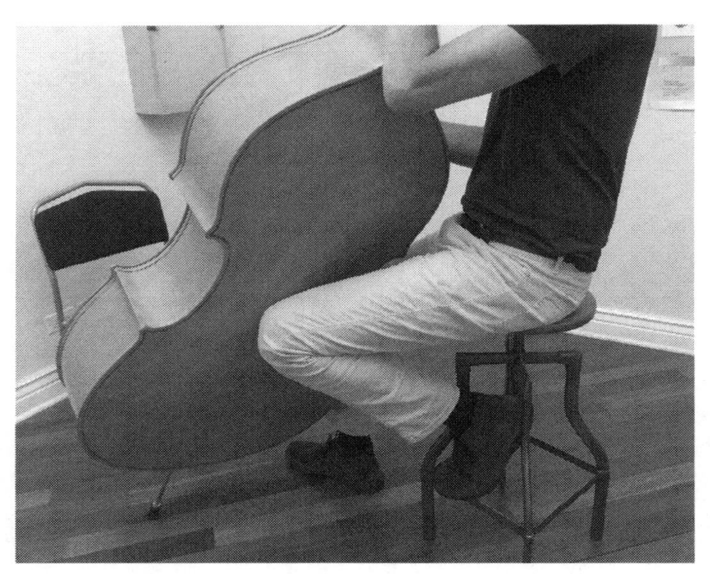

Figure 7. Placing one leg, most commonly the left, on the rung of a stool will cause the spine and pelvis to twist, which can cause back problems.

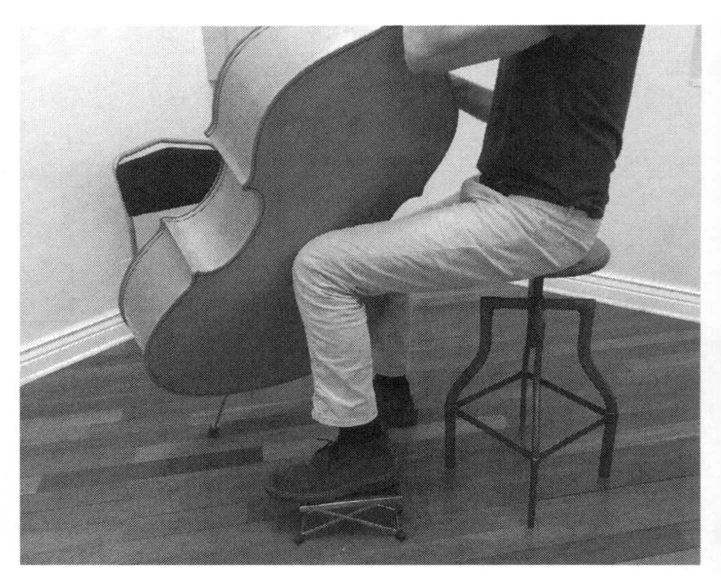

Figure 8. By placing the foot on a classical foot stool, or a yoga block, one can keep the pelvis stable and avoid twisting the back and pelvis, lessening greatly the chance of back problems.

This position also places extra pressure on the buttocks, and the aforementioned sciatica can develop which can compromise the piriformis muscle, creating local or radiating nerve pain traveling down into the leg.

A good compromise to the position previously described and shown in Figure 7 is to place the foot that one would rest on the rung of the stool, in the example in Figure 8 the left *(see figure 8)*, on a classical guitar pedal or now more commonly seen, a yoga block, which will reduce stress on the low back by placing the foot in a more natural position as it will now be flat rather than in a cocked back position. This will take the twisting and extra pressure off of the low back, pelvis, and buttocks. Sitting on a lower stool also will allow both feet to be placed flat on the floor, naturally, and will allow secure placement for the instrument, as well as giving one access to the fingerboard readily without having to reposition the instrument or the body.

Prevention: Postural Perspective

To help avoid injury from a postural perspective, a player can:

- foster awareness. Without your instrument, raise your shoulders upward as if you are trying to touch them to the bottoms of your ears, at the same time taking a deep breath in, and hold the shoulders and breath in this position for a few seconds. After a few seconds exhale through your mouth and drop your shoulders in a sudden motion and breath. You will notice that there is a release of tension, as the shoulders drop down a few inches from where they were just moments before and where they had been before you did the exercise. This means that much of the time we are walking around with our shoulders tensed up for no reason at all, and that it can be changed in a matter of seconds.
- remember to take a moment as you approach the instrument prior to playing to check your posture; weight should be equally distributed between both feet, shoulders relaxed, head and neck straight, spine straight rather than bent over.
- remember to check your relation to the instrument, bring it to you, not you to it. Check the angle of the bass resting on your body, ideally in more of an angled position on the abdomen, and make sure your endpin height is set so that you don't have to alter your posture unnecessarily to navigate the instrument or in compensation for tight muscles stemming from uncomfortable posture.
- whether standing or sitting, use the weight of the bass to one's advantage. If the bass is leaning against the body, into the fingers, the fingers do not have to press down as hard on the string and can be more relaxed and tension free.
- remember to employ economy of motion- more sound, less work.
- avoid looking at either the fingerboard or the right hand as much as possible, and when doing so come back to a neutral position, with the head up and relatively straight.

- avoid exaggerated movement as much as possible, and when doing so remember to come back to a more neutral position. This also applies to facial expressions, unnecessary bending over the instrument, and exaggerated bowing motions as well as leaning the head and neck forward excessively and too often, usually in time with the music.
- play on the same size instrument when practicing and performing, and in the same position, standing or sitting, whenever possible to avoid postural problems and unnecessary muscle tension that changes can bring.
- when seated, try to play on a stool that will allow you to keep both feet flat on the floor, which will reduce strain on the lower back and pelvis. If this is not possible, place the raised foot on a classical guitar pedal or yoga block to help reduce this strain.
- when seated, avoid sitting on the very edge of the stool to avoid compressing the piriformis muscles and sciatic nerve. Sit back more, remove items from your back pockets, and/or use a cushion.
- bend at the waist like a hinge when going into thumb position rather than straining the muscles of the low back.
- find and optimally start with a properly fitting and set up instrument, which will lessen the chance of muscle strain or injury and lessen the likelihood of posture problems due to fatigue.
- knowing the neck of the instrument up to thumb position will eliminate constant looking at the left hand, which can cause unnecessary neck and upper back tension to build up.

Left Hand/Side/Shoulder

When one is a double bass player, there are certain anatomical, physiological, and music making challenges that cannot be avoided except to recognize them and deal with them as best we can, trying to avoid potential causative factors for overuse and discomfort as much as possible in order to avoid pain in the short term and injury in the long term.

Let's start with the left hand and wrist.

When one plays the double bass, great strength of the left hand and lower arm is needed to press the strings down on to the fingerboard. Keeping the fingers curved uses muscles properly to press the strings down to the fingerboard, while playing with the fingers flattened or collapsed places extra stress and muscular tension on the fingers, hand, wrist, forearm, arm, and up to the shoulder and neck, which can cause one or multiple problems in this anatomic chain.

The thumb should not push excessively on the neck or squeeze the neck, as this will place unnecessary and cumulative stress on the thumb which can become problematic, sometimes sooner, sometimes later. The pressure from the thumb on the back of the neck should be equal to or less than that of the fingers on the fingerboard, that is, not excessive. The thumb should not be rigid or stationary, but follow the fingers as they move on the instrument, and not drag or get caught lagging behind, especially when shifting. The thumb should not bend back excessively from pressure, but have some flexibility; for those who are double jointed one must be aware of the extra motion afforded them and not press harder or allow the thumb to bend back more as this can easily cause problems in the thumb, hand and wrist area on the thumb side and possibly beyond. When approaching the instrument, rather than grabbing or gripping the neck, try placing the thumb on the back of the neck with little pressure and then wrap the fingers around the fingerboard and into position. In this way one can avoid excess pressure that could be applied to the thumb by a tense hand gripping the neck.

The left wrist should be kept straight (not rigid) as much as possible when not in service to the music or to a passage, and should not be overly flexed (bent), nor overextended, both of these potentially causing pain, unnecessary stress, and possible injury in the short or long term. Let the arm hang down at the side when possible, rather than hanging on the instrument maintaining tension when not in use. If the instrument is placed on the body properly, the left hand should not have to hold it up. Shake out the wrist if you feel unnecessary tension accumulating there.

Prevention: left hand/side/shoulder perspective

To help avoid injury on the left side, a player can:

- if a player has particularly small hands, one can go to thumb position sooner to avoid overstretching the thumb
- avoid cracking your knuckles. While the action itself is not injurious, as one is simply releasing gas which has built up in joints that are not moving at their full range of motion or are restricted, by repeating this action in a habitual way one can stretch the ligaments (structures which connect bone to bone) in the fingers to an extent where they become lax, or loose, from overstretching them. Once they are loose, a condition

called hypermobility, they cannot become tight again, so as cracking the knuckles is unnecessary, it should be avoided.

- avoid unnecessary raising of the shoulders when elevating the left arm, rather let the arm guide this motion as needed, without anticipating or exaggerating. While some positioning necessitates this motion, such as thumb position, remember once the need for this has passed so should the exaggerated, though necessary, motion. Raising the shoulder enlists back muscles to help with the motion, especially when prolonged or done habitually, and this can eventually cause long term problems in the back *(see figure 9)*.
- try and keep your fingers, wrist and forearm as free of tension as possible whenever possible. Only the finger playing a note should have tension, for example when the 1st finger is playing, the other fingers should be in a ready but relaxed position, not stretched out over the string. Let the thumb and other fingers release when they are not specifically playing, and hang loosely if not playing in general. Muscles in the forearm control movement in the hand and fingers, so unnecessary tension in one will affect the other.
- avoid collapsed fingers. If the joint of your finger collapses, one will resort to finger pressure and squeezing rather than natural arm weight, and this can result in injury.
- be careful when using devices to strengthen the hand and/or fingers, as this can easily promote overuse and cause injury.
- be careful not to squeeze the neck. Start with a loose grip for a better chance to end that way. Place the thumb on the back of the neck without excess tension and wrap the fingers around the fingerboard and into position to avoid gripping or grabbing the neck when getting ready to play.
- be careful to avoid holding the left arm up too high to avoid unnecessary tension.
- avoid overly bending the left wrist in flexion whenever possible to lessen tension in the arm and the possibility of wrist pain/injury.
- avoid overly bending the left wrist in extension whenever possible to lessen tension in the arm and the possibility of wrist pain/injury.
- bring the instrument to you, not vice versa, and don't hold the bass up with the thumb.
- avoid pressing down too hard on the strings with the left-hand fingers, as numbness can develop from pressing too hard for too long.

Figure 9. Avoid lifting the left shoulder when unnecessary to avoid arm/shoulder/neck/upper back discomfort. Try keeping the left shoulder as close to the body as possible without being rigid.

- when shifting, release the thumb, and avoid unnecessary shifts. Use the whole arm rather than excessively bending the wrist.
- don't hold chords longer than you need to, and release any abnormal hand positions as soon and as often as you are able.
- keep strings as low as possible, lowering the bridge to suit your technique and avoid pressing down on the fingerboard with unnecessary pressure causing unwanted tension and fatigue of the left hand. Try to consciously lighten your touch to find the optimal pressure. This is particularly important for younger players whose practices now will become future habits, and for older players who have arthritis and/or other joint issues.
- those who frequently play in the higher positions or who are of shorter stature should be careful when thrusting the left shoulder forward to avoid forearm

impingement when reaching down the neck, as this motion done repeatedly can cause inflammation or small tears in the shoulder joint or rotator cuff.

- avoid constant shoulder elevation, with the left arm out and up which makes one prone to rotator cuff problems and/or tendonitis in the shoulder.

Right hand/side/shoulder

With the right side, there are essentially two techniques and their associated motions bassists need to take note of, this being pizzicato and bowing. There are many advocates of both French and German bowing styles, and each has their advantages and drawbacks from an injury prevention perspective, as the two grips require different mechanics of the right hand, wrist, forearm, arm, and shoulder, and how each can affect the rest of the body.

Some commonalities among advocates and teachers of each style is the necessity of keeping the hand, wrist and arm as relaxed as possible, firm yet not rigid. The proper height for bowing is found by extending one's arm without locking the elbow and placing the bow in between the end of the fingerboard and the bridge without dropping the shoulder. If one has to drop the shoulder, this indicates the bass is not high enough and the end pin should be adjusted. One also should not have to bend at the waist to find this position.

The French bow has distinct technical differences from the German bowing style. The French bow is held with the right hand perpendicular to the stick of the bow. Problems come in with this style from the very start, as many tend to grab or grip the bow tightly and this becomes learned habit. One should hold the bow so as not to drop it, but also not squeeze it. When this hand position causes unnecessary tension and muscle tightness, this translates up the extremity and causes problems there, such as locking of the elbow, another problem.

German bow is quite different from French bowing in that the German bow is held from underneath in such a way that the force generated by the arm automatically directs the bow into the string. While straight, the right wrist should not be rigid, and should be as neutral or flat as possible and level with the forearm and top of the hand. The index finger is the main supplier of force, but is supported by the second finger and thumb. The little finger serves to hold up the bow and to direct it so that it moves at right angles to the strings. Bowing in this style should be done without pressure. Too much pressure by the bow against the strings will cause excess tension throughout the right arm. By closing the hand and keeping the fingers together and slightly curved, avoiding tensing up and gripping the bow unnecessarily rather than simply holding it, this will give good control over the German bow and help to avoid discomfort and injury.

It is generally felt that with the French bow, especially among beginners, pain, stiffness and fatigue are common symptoms. While this may likely be true to some extent, complete acceptance of this can lead to the establishment of bad habits due to compensation in one's technique to accommodate these issues, or the continuation of these symptoms ignored or tolerated by the player which can lead to injury if one is not mindful of them and/or some intervention is not attempted. It seems that with German bowing these issues are less prevalent, and less of a problem, which would explain its relative popularity.

When playing pizzicato, there are different fingering variations that one can use and different approaches to the style. Some feel it is best to pull with the entire arm rather than just the finger(s), as the finger will be weak when used alone and will call on other muscle groups to support it, creating unnecessary tension which will become habitual when repeated. Others feel that one should anchor the thumb on the side of the fingerboard and use only the fingers for pizzicato, giving the arm and shoulder a break from constant and repetitive motion. John Clayton believes it is fine to anchor the right thumb on the side of the fingerboard when playing jazz, and that in this position one can play towards the bridge or pivot the hand so that the fingers are parallel to the bridge, and one can play with two or three fingers in this fashion with the thumb in place as a constant. If one is playing strictly pizzicato, or playing for long periods, the best strategy is to alternate, using the whole arm in slow and less busy passages, and utilizing the hand and fingers when executing faster parts by anchoring the thumb on the side of the fingerboard and using a two finger technique. With either of these methods, take breaks when you can, dropping the arm and shoulder and shaking out the hand when possible. Shrug the shoulders when finishing a long passage and before starting another to keep them loose. When alternating bow and pizzicato, put the bow down when possible, especially in longer passages.

Prevention: Right hand/side/shoulder perspective

To help avoid injury on the right side, a player can:

- when bowing extend the arm without locking the elbow which should place the bow between the end of the fingerboard and the bridge. Adjust the bass height if you find you have to drop your shoulders to position the bow here, and don't bend at the waist to find this position.
- when bowing, regardless of the style, one should remember to keep the muscles of the bow hand and arm as relaxed as possible, maintaining only the amount of tension necessary to hold the bow and perform the task.
- keep the wrist level and stay relaxed, concentrating on just the weight of the arm. When beginning to draw the bow, remember to stay as relaxed as possible and avoid tensing up excessively and/or unnecessarily, keeping the bow level and perpendicular to the string.
- practice bowing without the bow at first, then with, then without the instrument, and then with, in front of the mirror when possible. This will help one to trouble-shoot and refine their bow hold, technique, and movement, especially as a beginner or when just learning a technique.
- when playing pizzicato, one can use the whole arm to avoid putting too much pressure on the hand and wrist, which can cause other muscles to become overutilized in compensation, and alternate by occasionally anchoring the thumb on the fingerboard and utilizing a two finger technique. Let the arm and shoulder hang down and shake out the hand when possible.
- when approaching a French bowing style, relax the arm, shoulder, and elbow before playing. Appropriate tension will manifest itself once playing begins, so to start in a relaxed position will help to keep initial tightness from becoming habitual.
- when approaching a German bowing style, position the bow in the web of the hand and let it hang down at the side while relaxing the arm. When raising the arm to play, don't raise with the wrist but rather rotate the forearm and wrist as one, keeping the wrist straight. Appropriate tension will manifest itself once playing begins, so to start in a relaxed position will help to keep initial tightness from becoming habitual.
- by playing harder, or louder, muscles tighten in response and excess tension results. Check the action on the instrument and evaluate your playing in general to see if you are expending too much energy with little return. Minimize effort for maximum results.
- when slapping on an upright, slapping, plucking, and striking the open hand on the fingerboard can all lead to carpal tunnel type syndromes. Take special care to stretch the hands and wrists properly before playing.
- be mindful of trying to maintain as neutral (without being rigid) a position in the hand, elbow, and shoulder as possible when possible, and to return to this neutral place whenever possible.
- when bowing, always remember to try and reduce excess tension from the very start. Tight muscles in the shoulder, arm, forearm, wrist, hand, and fingers all affect one another, in that order and vice versa, in any combinations thereof, with the weight being applied to facilitate this sequence starting in the muscles of the back. Don't hold the bow too tightly, commonly referred to as the "death grip". Don't squeeze the thumb when trying to hold the bow or to control one's volume. Don't press too hard on the stick with an overly curved thumb.
- keep the bowing arm as close to the body (yours and the body of the instrument) as possible, as the farther away from the body the arm is, the more it has to work to produce movement and to hold the arm and the bow up. This will produce tight musculature and can potentially cause tendonitis.

Electric Bass Technique

Following our earlier definition of technique, I have broken down into categories things I feel are important for a bassist to consider from an injury prevention perspective. The categories are Posture, Prevention from a Postural Perspective, Left Hand/Side/Shoulder, Prevention from Left Hand/Side/Shoulder Perspective, Right Hand/Side/Shoulder, and Prevention from Right Hand/Side/Shoulder Perspective. These categories represent a very basic overview, and further information on the conditions described and concepts covered are explored in greater detail elsewhere in this book and in *The Bassist's Guide to Injury Management, Prevention, & Better Health - Volume One.*

Posture

Considering this category of basses, the electric bass comes in a wide variety of shapes, sizes, weights, neck widths, scale lengths, and number of strings, all needing to be factored in to how one approaches the instrument from an injury prevention perspective, as well as how the instrument fits the player, such as how high on the body the bass is worn, what playing style is being used, what kind of straps one uses, and instrument set-up among other factors. Like the double bass, postural awareness is key for injury prevention purposes. Postural considerations include whether or not and when one should sit or stand, and the many factors that are involved in both positions. Other issues that come into play include how much you move around during a performance, and the constant repetitive movements of both extremities, the shoulders, arms, forearms, wrists, hands, and fingers, and how the spine responds to all of these factors.

Back pain is a concern to the bassist, and posturally there are many things that can cause this problem to arise. Electric bassists generally have a tendency to rotate the spine in a counterclockwise direction, causing the right shoulder to be thrust forward so that the forearm may be positioned at the front of the instrument. This can cause back pain due to the twisting of the spine. Is the issue the back twisting and thrusting the shoulder forward, or is the shoulder being thrust forward, due to a pose or postural habit, causing the back to turn? Either way, mid to low back pain and/or mid to upper back and shoulder pain and tightness can be the result. A forward and downward slope of the shoulders can cause neurologic symptoms, such as numbness and/or pins and needles, sometimes radiating into the extremities due to a usually transient impingement of nerves, or a pinched nerve.

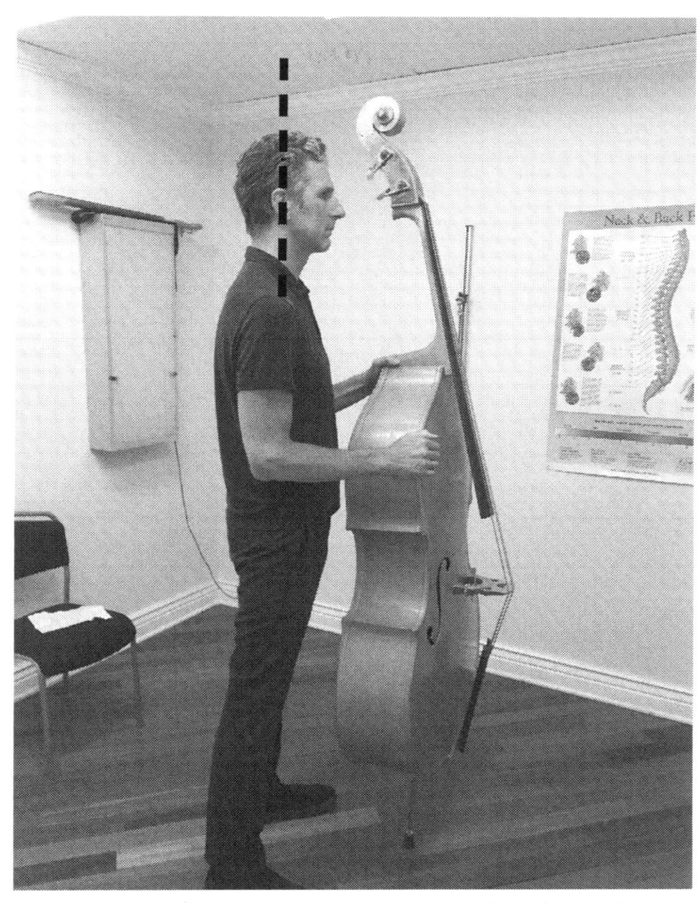

Figure 10. The concept of an imaginary string going from the top of your head to the ceiling can keep your head positioned correctly over your shoulders without raising the shoulders unnecessarily. It will also help to align the rest of your body properly underneath it.

Often this can be reversed through awareness and correction of posture such as pulling the shoulders back in a more erect position, or even better using the string attached to the top of the head strategy, as referred to in *The Bassist's Guide to Injury Management, Prevention & Better Health - Volume One,* whereby we pretend we have a string attached to the very top of our heads going up to the sky, and let that string pull us up by the top of our heads thereby straightening out the rest of our body along with it *(see figure 10).* This keeps the spine in an upright position and allows one's shoulders to drop back and relax, as when the head is pulled up the shoulders fall back naturally. As the shoulder and in turn the elbow function to move the arm and forearm respectively and position the hand in space and in relation to the instrument, the shoulder needs to be positioned properly in order for the rest of the extremity to be able to carry out its function to the best of one's ability. If the shoulder, on either side, is placed too far forward, back, and/or to the side, this can cause excess tension which again can translate into injury anywhere or everywhere along the extremity. One factor that can cause problems here is the inclination for most people, not just musicians, to slump forward, sitting or standing, especially in our case the bassist who slumps over their instrument while playing. This increases the curve of the spine in the middle, or thoracic area, which affects the positioning of the rib cage, with the shoulder blade then compensating by affecting the position of the shoulder, and so on down the extremity as just described.

Prevention

To help prevent injury from a postural perspective, a player can:

- avoid unnecessary and exaggerated movements of the shoulders, as this will create excess tension that can translate down the extremity to the arm, elbow, forearm, wrist, hand, and fingers, increasing the possibility of injury, contributing to a current problem, or forming new ones.
- avoid slouching or slumping forward over the instrument, as this causes distortions in the mid-back, or thoracic area of the spine, which will create tightness and tension in the neck and shoulder muscles and can become habitual, also sometimes producing neurologic symptoms which could become severe.
- avoid looking at either hand excessively or continuously while playing, as this can tighten and create excess tension in neck, shoulder and upper back muscles unnecessarily. Knowing the fingerboard of the instrument is a solution for the left hand, and as usual awareness is key to defeating this issue.
- select a strap that is wider than a normal guitar strap and which has some padding to avoid direct pressure on the shoulder from the instrument. That pressure will tighten up muscles in the neck and shoulder area, creating unnecessary tension and possibly leading to neurologic symptoms.
- many instruments now have chambering and use lighter woods and other alternatives, which produce a lighter instrument with usually slight if any changes in tone or sound production. Opting for one of these can create less tension on the neck, shoulders, and back when used instead of vintage or just heavier instruments.
- always wear your strap whether sitting or standing, and keep it at the same height so your body knows where the instrument is at all times and doesn't have to make unnecessary adjustments.

Figure 11. A classical foot stool (or yoga block) when sitting can help to keep the instrument at a proper height to avoid turning the back or lowering the neck/upper back when playing/practicing.

- avoid setting the strap height too high or low to avoid excess bending of either wrist, setting the stage for a repetitive stress type injury.
- when sitting, use a classical foot stool or yoga block to raise the left leg (if right handed) and rest the instrument on the left leg rather than the right to balance the pelvis properly and avoid twisting the back and/or slumping over the instrument *(see figure 11).* If the strap is set high enough, one can many times do without the foot stool/block as by wearing the strap it will sit on your body correctly and no adjustments need be made.
- warm up properly to avoid cramping up or injury.

Left hand/side/shoulder

A common place of playing related injury and pain is the fretting hand for electric bassists. This is not hard to imagine, as the fingers of the fretting hand are constantly performing small repetitive motions in a repetitive fashion, many times with less than optimal hand and wrist placement, creating tension which becomes learned habit over time and can work its way up the extremity, to the forearm, elbow, arm, shoulder and neck, upper back, or the opposite way, from the neck or shoulder on down and anywhere in between. Commonly the wrist

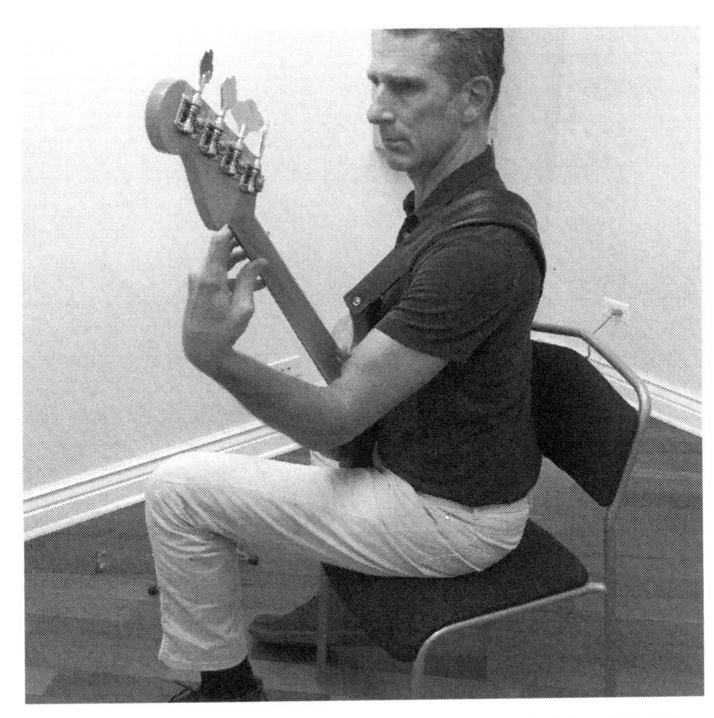

Figure 12. To avoid tendonitis and similar conditions, don't bend the left wrist (flexion) in an exaggerated fashion.

will be put in a position of excess flexion, or bending, to form chords and play passages, especially in the lower positions (those closest to the nut and headstock), or it can also be placed in excess extension, usually in the higher positions or toward the pick-ups or bridge, where the wrist is forced to flatten out or bend back *(see figure 12)*. Either of these positions decreases strength, which creates unwanted and added tension as one compensates by pressing harder, many times resulting in strain and/ or repetitive stress type injuries such as carpal tunnel syndrome. These types of injuries can occur in any style player, though there are some variances, usually stylistic and/or relating to posture and whether the player performs in a standing or sitting position.

Electric basses are to a large extent played in a standing posture and held essentially in a horizontal position or slightly above and supported by a strap, with the left hand depressing the strings directly against the fingerboard. For the player who plays seated, it is helpful to use a small stool, such as a classical footstool (or yoga block) under the left foot to elevate the knee, which places the instrument at a less horizontal and a more user-friendly angle. This angle helps the player keep the left wrist in a less acutely flexed state and in more of a neutral angle, which is easier on the wrist and extremity *(see figure 11)*. A pillow placed strategically and correctly in the lap can accomplish the same thing.

The genesis of many if not most bassists' injuries can be traced in some way back to the positioning of the wrists, affecting the hands and forearms, and the arms, affecting the forearms and shoulders, and the fact that these all interact with each other. Hand and finger size, along with the angle and height the instrument is being held at, are also factors. Players who play with the instrument lower on their body when standing, depending on playing style, can provoke extreme flexion of the fretting wrist and fingers, flexion meaning the wrist is bent towards the body with the fingers pointing up towards the player's head, or extension, in which the fingers are positioned lower than the wrist on the fingerboard. Time spent playing and the necessary repetitive motions involved in playing can mean the difference between these factors provoking injuries that are acute (new and short-term) and painful in the short run, or those that are chronic, learned activity, becoming career threatening injuries in the long run.

Muscles on the outside of the forearm, or extensors, move the fingers, lifting them off of the fingerboard away from the neck, while muscles on the inside of the forearm, or flexors, pull the fingers down onto the strings. These muscle groups contract, or tighten, when in use, which creates tension, and this is why through overuse excess tension is created which is how overuse or repetitive motion type injuries occur. Muscles in the hand allow for precise and fine movement, essentially placing the fingers where they need to go. When one of these muscle groups isn't operating in an efficient manner, through poor technique, weakness, or overuse, the other group of muscles (flexors or extensors) will have to work harder to compensate for the lack of production from the opposite muscle group, causing overuse type symptoms and potential injury in the second or compensating muscle group. In many cases a player will play through this pain hoping it will go away, creating habitual patterns that will plague them in the long run if not addressed and corrected early on.

As we have just stated, when the hand, wrist, and forearm are in positions of extreme flexion or extension, muscles can cramp up and cause pain. If a bassist is playing a repetitive figure in the same position, the muscles on the inside of the forearm (flexors) will place the pressure on the strings, and the muscles in the hand which flex the fingers will form the chord or figure. If the wrist is already in an overly flexed state, the muscles in the hand will shorten further to form the chord or figure, this position often causing pain and cramping in the hand and wrist due to muscle fatigue from excess tension and overuse of smaller muscles in the hand. These smaller muscles include the interossei, which abduct, or pull the fingers away from each other. Furthermore, if the flexor muscles are working by contracting to pull the fingers down to the fretboard, the extensor muscles on the other side of the forearm are stretching to allow this to happen. This works in reverse when taking the fingers off of the fretboard, as the extensor muscles are now working and the flexor muscles then will stretch to allow this to happen. The key to avoiding these exaggerated wrist positions is to try to keep the wrist in a more neutral, non-rigid position, neither overly flexed or extended, but somewhere in the middle of the two, while maintaining some fluidity of motion of the wrist itself. As it is impractical to have the wrist in a neutral position at all times, especially when playing, and undesirable for the wrist to maintain any kind of rigidity, if one can adopt a more neutral position whenever possible, and through awareness and technique lessen the usually exaggerated angles one utilizes when playing, it will be better for the player from an injury prevention perspective.

The positions of the fingers and their pressure on the strings when playing can be of concern to the electric bassist, as the repetitive motions of the fingers affect tendons, structures that attach muscles to bones, and can cause inflammation of these tendons, called tendonitis. The accuracy, precision and often rapidity necessary in playing, and the pressure on the individual to execute these movements can often cause one to press harder than necessary, and to not notice this due to the desire to get it right. Awareness of this issue will many times be enough to take care of the problem if one lightens up their finger pressure, or checks their instrument set-up including neck relief and action and adjusts them accordingly and if necessary.

Another common finding is when one places the thumb over the top of the fretboard in a position of flexion, whether to play notes, part of a chord, or for comfort or convenience in repetition. Keeping the thumb behind the neck in a relaxed position takes away unnecessary stress placed on the hand and thumb musculature (thenar muscles) by the aforementioned thumb over the top position. Squeezing with the thumb, whether over the top of the neck on the fingerboard or on the back of the neck can cause a condition called Dequervain's tenosynovitis, or Dequervain's syndrome, described in Chapter 2.

The left shoulder can also be a concern from an injury prevention perspective. As a general rule the left shoulder should support the arm as the arm simply hangs down in a neutral position and is held in the shoulder socket by ligaments and a tendon until it is called on for use. The elbow rests where it is tucked into the body just above the waist. From there, as we start to play, movement of the hand up and down the fretboard should be accompanied by minimal shoulder rotation and adduction/abduction (movement towards and away from the body respectively),

Figure 13. Keeping the strap on, when seated or standing, keeps the instrument at the same height and helps to avoid awkward seated posture which can have a detrimental effect on the back, pelvis, neck and shoulders. In this picture, a classical foot stool is also being used to help with optimal positioning of the instrument, but with the strap on and at a high enough height this is probably unnecessary, unless the player is playing for long periods of time, in which case the extra support is likely welcome.

which the elbow will naturally follow. The shoulder blade, or scapula, dictates the positioning of the upper arm and the hand, and the more the left shoulder deviates from a neutral position, the elbow will follow, and the greater the difficulty will be in placing the hand optimally on the fretboard (meaning in as neutral a position as possible, with only as much flexion and/or ulnar or radial deviation as necessary to complete the task). Therefore, where you place your hand on the fretboard affects the position of the shoulder. As we talk about neutral positioning, remember we are referring to the position as a reference only, as a place of not favoring or moving in any obvious direction, and not a state of rigidity or excess tension. There should only be as much natural tension in any movement as is necessary to perform the movement.

Holding the instrument on a strap over your shoulder affects superficial shoulder muscles such as the trapezius, and deeper shoulder muscles such as the levator scapulae. The size and positioning of the instrument, as in how high or low you wear it on your body, also affects the degree of elbow flexion, which can affect the shoulder, and sometimes will differ when sitting or standing depending on the postures you select. This is why I feel it is best to always keep the shoulder strap on, at the same height, whether sitting or standing to maintain as similar a position with your instrument as possible at all times. Other ways to handle this can be seen in the sitting and standing postures section of this chapter *(see figure 13).*

As we tend to carry stress in our neck and shoulder muscles, awareness of this issue and a compensatory mechanism is key. I suggest raising the shoulders up toward the ears consciously with a deep breath in, then letting them drop down, simultaneously exhaling through the mouth. This can be done several times during the day. The stress carried in the neck and shoulders causes their associated muscles to respond by tightening and shortening, raising the shoulders up higher where this stress becomes constant and accepted as "normal" behavior by the body, keeping the shoulders in this raised position. Thus, having this tension in the neck and shoulders becomes a learned behavior, unless one is aware of this and does an exercise like the one described above to relieve this tension and keep it from accumulating.

Commonly in both standing and sitting position, especially if one is doing a lot of work on a laptop or any computer or leaning forward to see a music stand, there is a tendency for the shoulders to slump downward and forward, and this slope of the shoulders and arms may produce symptoms of nerve compression, such as numbness and/or tingling in the arms. This feels like a radiating sensation coming down from the neck and/or shoulder, partially or all the way to the fingers, and in many cases by correcting this slump and straightening out one's posture this will go away. An example of a strategy for this can be seen in the posture section of this book, or in more detail in the Posture section of *The Bassist's Guide to Injury Management, Prevention, & Better Health - Volume One.*

Prevention

To help prevent injury on the left side, a player can:

- avoid placing the wrist in awkward exaggerated positions as much as possible, for example excessive flexion (bending the wrist so that the fingers point toward the face), extension (with the wrist higher than the fingers on the fretboard) or ulnar or radial deviation, in which the wrist bends to the side toward the pinky or thumb side respectively. Try to keep the wrist in as neutral (straight) a position as possible, whenever possible, but not rigid. For example, one can't play with a straight wrist, but one also usually doesn't have to bend the wrist as much as they do, and when not playing one can put the wrist in a neutral yet fluid position and/or shake it out to break habitual patterns which could cause repetitive stress type injuries.
- warm up- I find it best to start at the bottom of the neck (by the pickups) where the frets are closer together and work your way up to the head stock, as this increases blood flow and stretches the hands and forearms naturally before working your way up to larger stretches of the fingers and larger frets.
- before and after playing and periodically during the day take a deep breath in, at the same time raising the shoulders up toward the ears, and exhale through the mouth, dropping the shoulders down simultaneously. This will help to relax the neck and shoulders and rid them of any excess tension that may have developed there.
- don't let the thumb lag behind when shifting positions on the neck, as that can cause unnecessary strain in the thumb. Also, try to refrain from placing the thumb over the top of the neck, or squeezing the neck when playing as this can also cause problems in the thumb and its surrounding area.
- refrain from digging in too much when playing, as this can unnecessarily strain hand muscles. Playing lightly and turning up the volume on the amp to compensate will lessen strain on the hands and improve economy of motion and dexterity. Lowering the action on the instrument can also help, relieving the pressure that comes from pressing high strings down to the fretboard in a repetitive fashion. Lighter gauge strings can also help in this regard.
- It helps if one arches their fingers when playing, as this allows the strength generated by the forearm muscles to pass efficiently to the fingertips without being impeded.
- If the bass is worn very low it will put the left hand into excess flexion or extension causing cramping and pain.
- try to avoid having the shoulder out to the side, rather try to keep it and the arm closer to the body, but not rigidly, to avoid problems in the shoulder area.

Right hand/side/shoulder

The right hand, side and shoulder of electric bassists will have unique challenges from an injury prevention perspective.

One issue is that the instrument is typically strung with fairly heavy weight strings. Being thicker than guitar strings, these strings require greater effort in the case of the left hand to depress them against the fingerboard, or in the case of the right hand, which we are discussing

Figure 14. Bending the wrist in excess flexion can cause tendonitis, carpal and/or ulnar tunnel syndromes. A common mistake/cause of this comes from resting the forearm or wrist on the instrument unnecessarily. Ulnar tunnel problems are exacerbated when one angles the wrist towards the pinky in addition to flexion. Anchoring the thumb on the pickup keeps the wrist/hand rigid, making this already bad positioning even worse.

here, to pluck, pull, or pick them. This can cause right sided problems such as pain in the back of the hand (usually in the form of a carpal bone restriction), tendonitis, or conditions such as carpal tunnel or ulnar tunnel syndrome, as a player may have to dig in more, resulting in the need to use greater force, change their wrist angle, or make some other type of modification to get the appropriate response from the instrument. As regards plucking, the index finger is better able to handle and manage pressure on the string and the tension of the string in general, because it is stronger than the other fingers. If a player's technique is already being compromised by another factor such as resting their forearm on the instrument, anchoring on the pickups, or angling their wrist in extreme flexion to name a few possibilities, the extra tension created by this increase in pressure could mean the player is setting themselves up for potential short or long term injury. Lighter gauge strings are available, and using these may provide a solution to a bassist's hand problems, but this may come with an unsatisfactory compromise in desired sound quality. If a player lightens their touch on the instrument, turning up the volume on the amplifier or on the instrument itself, the electronics do the work, not as much effort needs to be exerted for the same sound, and many of these issues can be avoided. Lowering the action on the instrument and/or adjusting the neck relief can also help to lessen the pressure being placed on the fingers, hand and wrist when playing, and can help to avoid pain and injury.

The electric bass is usually played standing, with the instrument held almost horizontally and partly supported by a thick neck strap. If a bassist flexes their wrist to pluck the strings and practices or gigs this way for a good length of time, the right volar (palm) side forearm muscles shorten little by little, causing them to tighten up which to the body becomes a learned behavior over time. The shortened muscles place stress on tendons that are already working harder to play in a repetitive fashion, and the tendon sheaths that lubricate the tendons and the tendons themselves can become inflamed because of this additional tension and stretching, resulting in tendonitis after years of similar repetitive activity.

Tendonitis at the wrist, involving tightening of muscles known as the flexor carpi ulnaris, flexor carpi radialis, and extensor carpi ulnaris, is most commonly seen among electric bass guitarists. When in playing position, the flexor carpi ulnaris muscle flexes and bends the hand sideways toward the pinky. The flexor carpi radialis flexes and bends toward the thumb, while the extensor carpi ulnaris goes in the opposite direction, bending the hand back and then towards the pinky. As an electric bass player, both hands will perform constant repetitive motions. The right, with constant plucking or picking, will be most affected in the motions of flexion and ulnar deviation, in other words, bending the wrist down and sideways toward the pinky *(see figure 14)*. These motions make tendonitis more likely and will stress the flexor carpi ulnaris tendon in particular which will cause pain and/or cramping in that area. Sometimes with tendonitis, a misalignment or improper function of a larger group of muscles causes increased demand on smaller groups of muscles. For example, problems with hands or arms can often be traced back to the neck or shoulders. Tightness in the muscles related to those areas can pinch nerves which travel down the arm and supply the arms, forearms, and hands. This can also work in reverse, as tightness in the wrist or forearm areas can cause muscles to tighten and send pain radiating upward, back along the length of the involved muscle.

Again, excessive flexion of either the right or left hands is the special problem of the bass player. Try to keep the hands in more of a neutral position, not bending too far forward or backward, instead of the excessive bend at the wrist that most of us seem to gravitate to with both our right and left hand technique. Lowering the action on the instrument and/or checking the neck relief can help with right hand pain produced by having to pluck too hard, or with left hand discomfort caused by repetitively pressing down on strings raised unnecessarily high off of the fretboard.

Prevention

To help prevent injury on the right side, a player can:

- refrain from digging in too much, as this can unnecessarily strain hand muscles. Playing with a lighter touch and turning up the volume on the amp and/or instrument to compensate is a solution to this issue. This will lessen strain on the hands and improve economy of motion and dexterity. Lowering the action on the instrument and/or adjusting neck relief will also help, relieving right hand plucking or picking tension. Lighter gauge strings can also help in this respect.
- when practicing for extended periods of time, take breaks, avoid gripping too much, play different things in a different order and/or to different tempos to minimize repetition, and stretch and shake out your hands and wrists when necessary.
- avoid resting the forearm on the instrument *(see figure 14)*, which creates tension in the extensor muscles of the forearm and which can lead to other conditions, frequently ulnar tunnel syndrome, medial epicondylitis (golfer's elbow), and/or lateral epicondylitis, otherwise known as tennis elbow (see *The Bassist's Guide to Injury Management, Prevention & Better Health - Volume One* Conditions chapter for more details on these common issues for the bassist). Your hand will be more relaxed once you get it off the instrument completely.
- when playing with a pick, grip with a relaxed hold between the thumb and index finger, stabilized by the middle finger. This will help to reduce unnecessary tension in the hand, wrist, forearm, and on up the limb to the neck if severe enough.

These categories represent a very basic overview, and further information on the conditions described and concepts covered are explored in greater detail elsewhere in this book and in *The Bassist's Guide to Injury Management, Prevention, & Better Health - Volume One.*

CHAPTER FOUR

Inspiration Information

The following musicians and experts in their fields have graciously donated their time, thoughts and expertise to the author and this book. They have a lot to say and have my gratitude for their participation and generosity.

Ariane Cap

Ariane Cap is a multi-instrumentalist, educator, author, blogger, and composer. An eclectic and versatile bassist, she has covered many styles, and is an online teaching personality with a thriving blog and bass courses and webinars that draw a loyal following. Her book, *Music Theory for the Bass Player* is a frequent bestseller on Amazon. You can find out more about her at www.arisbassblog.com and www.arianecap.com.

Q: As a female player, are there any specific problems or issues that you may experience on a regular basis or that you have experienced that may be gender specific? What did or do you do about them?

A: If you asked me this question a while back, I would have given an answer that centered around being the recipient of negative bias as a female bassist. And yes, there were the occasional snarky remarks, such as:
"We need a real bass player, Honey" (hangs up the phone).
"Let me feel your callouses!" (grabs my hand).
"Oh come on, I need the guy who will actually be playing the instrument" (the sound guy as we all line up for sound check).

The constant grouping with other female bass players as if we were some sort of different class of bassists really bothered me at times. Attempts to compliment sometimes failed as in "You are amazing for a woman!"

I have encountered prejudice from men and women alike. I have met women who want to be the only woman in the band. I once did not get past the audition because the one female band member was irritated that I was younger than her. On the other hand, I have met women who do not want to play in all-female projects for fear of appearing weak or enhancing any bias against women.

All that said, I have had overwhelmingly positive interactions in the industry, and it is easy to lose sight of that over a few negative encounters! I work with incredible musicians, industry representatives, and collaborators (from stage to studio to tech to PR and endorsements); women and men of many backgrounds. My students trust me deeply. I cherish teaching in all sorts of settings, including with a group of female teachers who teach Jazz exclusively to girls and women (wonderful role modelling!) Professionals and mentors I greatly admire invite me to teach at their seminars. I am grateful for this; I really don't want to dwell on the few bad apples whose attitude just showed their ignorance, not mine.

The biggest problem with focusing on negative experiences is that we can start internalizing them. In some co-creating situations I still catch myself disregarding my creative voice or retreating from actively shaping the music, because I am afraid to invade someone else's space or to not have something worthwhile to offer. I sometimes over-prepare and overwork myself because I think just showing up and doing my thing might "not be enough". I have colleagues (male and female) who will catch that and encourage my voice, which of course shows they can relate.

Other than bias, there is a social aspect in band dynamics that can take some navigating as a woman. The guys sometimes fear they can't be themselves when a woman is in the band van and that they have to watch their jokes. Logistics like extra hotel rooms can become an issue. There is the assumption that women always stick together, and any kind of road romance will get immediately and eagerly spread by the female to their girlfriends or wives (oh, please!).

I have found that by being professional and fun to be around, and by being a team player and all about the music, those things become a non-issue fast, if you are touring with the right people.

When networking with other musicians I have run into situations where I couldn't be sure whether I was asked for my card for personal or business reasons.

Reversely, on one occasion I asked a pianist for his info because I really liked his playing and he said 'Oh no, I am married!'. (I really did mean his piano playing, and being a bassist was not a pick-up line!)

Sometimes people assume there may be specific physical issues that can hold back a female bass player. This is categorically not true in my experience. Playing a powerful groove comes from excellent technique and a clear vision for the song, not any kind of strength or muscle size. The girls have zero disadvantage there!

Q: As an educator, what mistakes do you notice most in a player's technique?

A: Too much unnecessary movement in both hands, as well as lack of coordination between left and right. This leads to seemingly insurmountable roadblocks, speedbumps, sloppy tone and bad timing. I also see a lot of players squeeze the neck with their left hand, thereby creating unnecessary tension all over the body. I help them to be as relaxed as possible when they play so the music can flow through them.

Over-gripping, pulling up a shoulder or tensing one's neck are unconscious habits that take a bit of careful practicing to change for good. I have spent a lot of time developing methods to transform those pesky habits for myself and others.

Also, developing great fingering habits in the fretting hand and working the right hand effectively really pays off - practicing scales according to positions on the bass - not only from root to root - is great; as is including shifts and jumps between positions all across the fretboard. In the method I developed we practice everything over the whole fretboard and in all keys. This is a very systematic approach with the goal to free up the mind to focus on the music; the fingers can find their way comfortably, always positioned toward the direction of what comes next. My practice routines also incorporate a big mental practice piece (training away from the instrument). The goal is to think ahead and listen inside the mind. I find it frees up my creativity a lot.

Q: Any special road or studio tips?

A: For studio gigs (and general playing, really) I recommend to practice using recording software. Seeing those metronome clicks or drum beats on one track and the bass (attacks, note lengths, dynamics) on the other really drives home any kind of inconsistency in the playing. Seeing the dynamic or timing fluctuations zoomed in and magnified provides a sense of reality and sharpens one's hearing. Can you hear or see first what's up exactly? The experience of listening back intensely to short phrases that one just played can be very illuminating and really make you look at your phrasing, timing, fingering and technique.

And a tip for the road: eat healthy and keep your body moving. I belong to 24 Hour Fitness, so if the hotel does not have a fitness studio, I usually find a 24-hour facility somewhere. I go jogging in a pinch.

Q: Any special tips or general advice you would like to share with other players?

A: Aim high and expect the best of yourself. Have a regular practice routine. Be your own coach. Surround yourself with supportive musicians who know you well and respect you. Don't buy into bleak and cynical voices about the state of the music industry. If you remain open to the demands of your fans and flexible to the ever-changing landscape of media, you will do well.

And feel free to do your own thing. Take it from someone who taps on the six string and has a duo with a bassoon player (!) - if you follow your heart, your authenticity will connect with people.

Thank You Ariane!

Ed Friedland

Ed Friedland has been at the forefront of bass education for over 30 years, having written 20 instructional books for Hal Leonard. As a columnist and contributing editor for Bass Player magazine, Ed has written hundreds of instructional articles, many compiled in his book, "The Working Bassist's Toolkit." As a performer, Ed crosses all stylistic boundaries with his fluency on upright and electric bass, and he is currently touring bassist with The Mavericks. In addition to teaching and performing, Ed has cultivated a rabid following of bass gear enthusiasts through his work as "The Bass Whisperer." Ed Friedland's Road Report can be seen at www.bassmagazine.com, and The Bass Whisperer can be seen on his YouTube channel BassWhispererTV.

Q: As a working bassist, educator, and industry vet, are there any specific problems from an injury perspective that you have experienced or that you experience on a regular basis?

A: I personally have experienced at least three bouts of tendinitis over the span of 30 years that required me to take a break from playing.

Q: What did or do you do about it?

A: I've tried just about everything out there! And honestly, I've had success with a lot of things. The obvious things like applying ice as soon as you're injured, or right after you play, staying hydrated, gentle stretching, taking arnica, are all good daily maintenance. But in the midst of a flare up, I'll use chiropractic, acupuncture, ultrasound, physical therapy in addition to the other things mentioned. The real key is learning to stay relaxed in your body while you play. Then - no more problems!

Q: As a player who plays upright and/or doubles frequently, are there any special things to be aware of when playing the upright bass, or when switching frequently between upright and electric, whether in a single night or for different gigs on consecutive nights?

A: The upright takes more physical strength to play, but that doesn't necessarily mean you have to fight it. I work with the tension of the instrument, not against it. But proper setup is a big factor. A poorly setup bass can really screw up your hands. Switching to electric, it's important to relax into it, and realize that you don't need the same level of strength to produce a note. And, it's not just about playing the thing, people have injured themselves just picking it up!

For the actual switch on the gig, I've set it up so I can put one bass in the stand, grab the other, and return to playing position in a circular movement. It's an ergonomic sequence that works with my stage space. Sometimes I have to switch without notice, very quickly. Having it dialed in to a smooth sequence of movements makes it an automatic response... no stress, just a smooth, circular movement.

Q: Also, you have used different versions of upright basses on the road over the years, including a Chadwick travel bass and an Azola Baby Bass; have these helped in avoidance of injury, and if so how?

A: The basses haven't contributed anything in particular, it's more a matter of how they are setup to play. The Azola Baby Bass is a little easier to play, but again, that's setup.

Q: Are there any special concerns you are aware of from an injury prevention perspective associated with playing 5 or 6 string basses, or specialized playing such as plucking/thumping/tapping or playing with a pick?

A: My first bout with tendinitis came after furiously shedding on a 6-string for a high profile gig... the initial adjustment from 4 to 6 strings should be taken slowly! The width of the neck, the stress from not knowing where the hell you are on the neck—it makes for a very tense experience at first. Tension = problems. As far as other techniques, again, it's all about noticing and managing the level of tension in your body as you play. It helps to breathe, keep your toes flexible, loosen the shoulders.

Q: In your experience in many aspects of playing and the industry, what mistakes from an injury prevention perspective do you notice most when watching other players, or what conditions do you most see or hear about in other players?

A: If I had a dollar for every bass player I've heard about with tendinitis! It seems that repetitive movements, over long periods of time, at long scale lengths is a recipe for trouble! But when you see long-time pro players, they've usually gone through the fire and figured out how to do their thing without hurting themselves. You can't sustain a pro career otherwise.

Q: Any special tips or general advice for players, studio, road, or otherwise?

A: Stay loose, stay hydrated. Have fun, but know your limits. Take care of yourself, someone has to play the bass.

Thank You Ed!

Stuart Hamm

Stuart Hamm is perhaps best known for his recording and touring roles with guitar legends such as Steve Vai and Joe Satriani. However, for serious students of the electric bass, Hamm's influence and impact on the instrument are far more extensive. Regarded as one of the most technically gifted bassists to have emerged out of the jazz/rock genre in the last thirty years, Hamm has released a string of impressive solo albums, along the way becoming an ambassador for virtuoso bass playing through his mastery of slap and pop techniques and his pioneering work with two handed tapping and solo bass playing. Visit him at www.stuhamm.com.

Q: Are there any specific problems you may experience on a regular basis or that you have experienced as a player from an injury or pain related point of view?

A: After years of nonstop touring with Satriani, my own band, GHS, and the Mexican pop band Caifanes, I had such incredible pain in my right wrist that I stopped playing for a few months and then played with a brace on my right wrist/hand.

Q: What did or do you do about it?

A: Billy Sheehan recommended that I see a chiropractor friend of his and this started my long association with chiropractic, yoga, breathing and "alternative" medicine and healing… I had 3 'doctors' give me 3 different diagnoses...It turned out that I had a reverse out "military" curve in my neck that was stopping the flow of energy and blood correctly, and it affected my whole body, mainly manifested in my wrist.

Q: With your unique combination of playing styles, especially your distinctive tapping style, are there any special concerns to be aware of with these styles as regards possible injury that may occur?

A: It's very important to take the time to warm up and stay relaxed. A very curved left hand is needed to tap the strings down at a 90 angle to get the right tone and clarity. A very pianistic approach, but when I tried to go back and actually try to work up some of my old piano repertoire, I found that the muscles used were very different and I wasn't able to switch back and forth.

Q: Any special road tips?

A: Don't eat crappy food. Don't drink too much. Don't over medicate....meditation and breathing work and yoga actually make you feel better in the long run than booze and pills. Don't try to fight jet lag. If you wake up in Japan at 3 a.m., read or meditate, just rest and don't stress about trying to fall asleep when your body clock is awake. Don't be annoying and talk too much on the bus/van. Give everyone their space and be respectful.

Q: Any special studio tips?

A: I have my bass up SO LOUD in the playback mix I hear when I record, that it forces me to play very lightly, which ends up providing a more even and better sounding bass track than if you are playing too hard. Actually, the harder you play, the less low end you will get.

Q: What mistakes do you notice most in a player's technique that could cause possible short or long term injury?

A: Too many to list here... but everyone is different. I would just say that if you are playing, and something HURTS, then stop, shake it out and start RIGHT NOW seeing what you can change... posture... strap height to width... to enable you to play without any pain. It should NEVER hurt.

Q: Any advice, tips or exercises you want to share with players?

A: Remember to develop a good warm up routine that you do EVERYTIME before you play… Renaldo or LeBron would not walk out of the car onto the pitch or court and just start playing… you need to warm up. If you develop a routine you will find yourself doing it without even thinking about it. Remember to BREATHE and RELAX!

Thank You Stuart!

Chris Jisi

Chris Jisi is a New York City-born and based professional bassist and music journalist. After getting his first bassist interview published in *Guitar Player* in 1982, he continued to write about bass players for GP, *Guitar World, Musician, Drums & Drumming* and other music publications, until landing a staff writer position with *Bass Player* magazine upon its inception in 1990. Having spent the ensuing years interviewing a who's who of bassists for BP, Chris was named Editor in Chief of *Bass Player* in April 2014. Along the way, he has released two collections of his interviews, *Brave New Bass*, in 2003 and *The Fretless Bass*, in 2008. He currently is senior editor at www.bassmagazine.com.

Q: As a working bassist with a day job that involves lots of typing, computer work, etc., you are potentially more susceptible to developing conditions such as tendonitis, carpal tunnel, etc. Are there any specific problems you may have experienced or that you have on a regular basis related to pain or injury, and do you attribute that more to one occupation or the other or do they overlap? What did or do you do about it?

A: I am on the desktop computer a lot, a good chunk of most days. I've been fortunate that it hasn't affected my back or my hands/arms, especially related to playing. What it HAS done is (along with the aging factor, I'm 60) ruin my eyes. I use reading glasses to read papers, my iPad, sometimes my phone, but not the desktop (where you can just make things bigger).

Q: Are there any special concerns as a five & six string player, pick player, or upright player that you notice?

A: I mainly play nicely spaced 5-strings (Sadowsky, Fodera) so no problem switching to 4-string. However, if I play a tight 5-string. I feel it in both hands afterward (I guess muscle soreness or cramping because I'm not used to that spacing). For a period, about ten years ago, I was playing a BMX 38" - scale electric upright. I don't recall any problems even though it was upright and with a much fatter neck.

Q: As someone who knows, has interviewed, and has seen every important bassist in our lifetime, are you aware of any conditions that are more prevalent amongst players, or that are potentially career threatening? If so, do you know how they overcame or deal with these issues?

A: Honestly, I haven't paid close enough attention. I feel like back problems are the most mentioned, with different strap configurations as the solution. Next would be carpal tunnel from over-practicing or playing. Seems like the solutions have ranged from surgery and icing to just laying off playing the instrument for a long spell. I always recommend your book!

Q: What mistakes from an injury prevention perspective do you most notice in a player's technique?

A: Hmmm, I'm no expert and I'm not actively looking, but through your book and heightened awareness of the physical side of playing, I cringe when I see someone whose plucking hand is folded at the wrist, with their arm tucked in (I just think of all the circulation and nerves being cut off at the wrist). Not related to injury specifically, but when the plucking hand thumb curls up and over the fingerboard that always seems improper to me and a poor ergonomic choice. Also the height that players wear their bass seems key. Many punk and rock bassists seem to wear basses too far down, which can result in both hands having to be at an angle that can cut off circulation (especially the fingering hand). On the other hand (no pun), when the fusion guys started wearing their basses very high, that can cut off plucking hand circulation, as I spoke about above. I wear mine in the middle.

Q: Based on this wealth of experience, do you have any special tips, exercises, or general advice for players from an injury prevention perspective?

A: I wish I had more experience related to injury prevention. Mainly I'd point to what I mentioned above, not curling the hands, and wearing the bass at a suitable height. Posture is a biggie, and I see a lot of bassists with a slouch, so I guess being conscious of standing up straight, with your chest out and your stomach in. I would recommend warming up before you play, slowly to get everything lubricated before trying anything too crazy. Stretching or cracking the fingers never sit right with me.

Here are some other things that come to mind:

1) I tend to remember the recent interviews the best. That said, I've always regarded Gary Willis as having a real well-thought out approach to technique, where the coordination between hands is the key, and the way he approaches string skipping and assigns certain fingers to certain strings. Victor Wooten has well-thought out technique as well, even with all of his radical approaches. In my *Bass Player* cover story on Carlitos Del Puerto the following passage caught my ear: "On both instruments I focus on coordination exercises. It's not about speed on bass, it's about coordination. Everyone has one hand that's faster than the other. For me, my left hand is faster, so I've always worked on getting my right hand to the same speed. Equally important is getting both hands to the same level of endurance, especially on the upright."

2) My playing profile and physical condition might be of some help: I mainly play in my 12-25 piece wedding band, mostly on weekends. At this point we mainly play weddings and corporate parties for those at the top of the wealth chain, traveling to gigs about 35% of the time. It's true music by the pound (dance music from all eras). Wedding and party planners don't want a pause in the music, so often I'll be playing four hours straight, with one or no breaks. Because my biggest problem is bad knees(I pounded the cartilage out of both knees from playing basketball on concrete playground courts my whole life, and I had my right knee replaced) I sit on a high padded stool, usually with a back. But my back can get sore at times from the weight of sitting plus having the bass on my lap (though strapped on). That will lead me to stand up for a few songs. If I don't play all week or we have two weeks off, I notice my hands can get sore; mostly my plucking hand fingertips, if the calluses get too soft, and in my right hand, in the muscle between my index finger and thumb.

Thank You Chris!

Dino Monoxelos

Dino is a graduate of Musicians Institute (BIT) and in 1991, after graduating, was asked to join the faculty. There he studied with Bob Magnusson, Putter Smith, Jeff Berlin, Gary Willis, Steve Bailey, Alexis Sklarevski, Jim Lacefield and Tim Bogert to name just a few, and since he's been back in Boston, Bruce Gertz.

He is the author of four books to date, *Odd Meter Bassics* (MonoTunes Music), "Essential Styles for Bass" (Mel Bay), *Mastering the Fingerboard* (Mel Bay), and *Electric Bass for the Young Beginner* (Mel Bay) as well as being the featured artist for the Mel Bay DVD, *Bass Chords Made Easy*. He has been a longstanding columnist for both *Bass Frontiers* magazine and *Bass Guitar Magazine*.

Dino is also the Ampeg Brand Marketing Manager, and has affectionately become known in the bass community as "The Ampeg Guy" for the last sixteen years. Conducting in-store and in-school clinics and appearances around the world as well as numerous YouTube and Google Video instructional videos for Ampeg has been his goal for the last 8++ years. Find out more and visit him at www.monotunesmusic.com.

Q: As a working bassist, educator, and industry vet, are there any specific problems you have experienced or that you may experience on a regular basis?

A: Yes. I have a condition called Essential Tremor. It's a neurological condition that causes a rhythmic trembling or "shaking" of the hands, head, voice, legs, or trunk. In my case it affects my hands. It's sometimes confused with Parkinson's disease although it's eight times more common, affecting an estimated 10 million Americans and millions more worldwide. I've had it since I was a kid and never knew what it was. My dad had it and my older brother has it. Only until recently I did an internet search on "shaky hands" and all of this info on Parkinson's and ET came up. That led me to seeing my doctor about it who eventually diagnosed me with ET a number of years back.

I've also had back problems since I was a teenager that have gotten worse over the years. Lifting, carrying, and standing for long periods of time with a bass strapped around my neck hasn't really helped my condition either which is probably true for most musicians. At my age now, I've been diagnosed with stenosis which is basically a narrowing of the nerve cavities in my vertebrae which the nerves pass through. This can sometimes be pretty painful and frustrating, especially when standing or performing for long periods of time too. Not to mention lifting and lugging heavy bass gear around..

Q: What did or do you do about it?

A: As for the ET, well, I read about it and did my own "research", as well as joined a couple of online and Facebook support groups to see how others deal with it. My doctor also prescribed a drug called Propranolol which helps with my ET as well as high blood pressure. The problem with Propranolol though is it eventually becomes less and less effective and you have to increase the dosage. Unfortunately because it also affects blood pressure, I can't increase my dosage much more. Plus it comes with some other side effects like constant tiredness and fatigue. My next stop was to look at my diet and exercise routine. Diet has a LOT to do with EVERY aspect of one's health no question!

In my case, trying to stay off caffeine and any kind of stimulants such as sugar and white starches always helps. Alcohol, though its initial effects are useful, doesn't help because the next day, most of that alcohol translates into sugar and I'm right back to where I started and in some cases worse. Plus, I can't be walking around drinking all the time... or maybe I can? LOL!

I also found that foods rich in magnesium as well as magnesium supplements helps quite a bit. I even have magnesium oil that I rub into my hands and wrist twice a day that does seem to quell my tremors quite a bit. It's amazing how people don't realize how deficient they are in certain very important vitamins and minerals. Magnesium is one of those minerals that is vital to us in so many ways. Vitamin D is another one that we found. My younger daughter is vitamin D deficient and it affects her in so many ways as well. Thank God my wife works for a vitamin company. I've gotten a lot of my vitamin/mineral knowledge from her and her co-workers.

Anyway, diet and exercise definitely helps with my condition more than anything. As for my stenosis and back pain, I've been getting help through chiropractic care but also exercise and diet have a lot to do with it too. Obviously less weight on my back means less weight to carry around. I've also had steroidal injections in my lower back which help with the inflammation. But, each time the injections become less and less effective and don't last as long as the last. Eventually I might have to have surgery to try to open up those narrowing passageways. I'm thinking that will definitely be a LAST resort. The thought of someone cutting into my back is just terrifying! (Ed. note: Dino has since this interview had surgery to correct this condition, which shows that despite one's best efforts sometimes this is the only/best solution).

Q: Are there any special concerns you are aware of from an injury prevention perspective associated with playing 5 or 6 string basses, or specialized playing such as plucking/thumping/tapping, upright playing, or playing with a pick?

A: Oh boy... where do I start? I guess in general, my approach to all of these concerns is proper playing technique mostly. Whether you're playing a 4, 5, 6 or 20 string bass, or using any of the aforementioned playing techniques, I think it's really REALLY important to watch, listen, and FEEL how your body, specifically your wrist and hands react to all of this.

Next I'd say your upper body, neck, shoulders and back just from supporting a heavy instrument for so many hours a day or performance. If you're playing in such a way that it just doesn't feel comfortable right from the start, change it right away to something that IS more comfortable. Strap height, position of the instrument ON your body, weight of the instrument, angle of your arms, wrists and hands are all very important. And because our bodies are all different, there's no "right" way to do it. Do what feels most comfortable to you. And experiment until you do find what's most comfortable.

I actually DO play a 5 string bass primarily, as well as thumping, tapping, plucking, playing with a pick AND play upright. All of that on top of my ET, I'm a hand surgeon's dream! Seriously, have you ever just looked at another bass player's hands? It's amazing to see, the actual deformities in some of our friend's hands from playing bass for so many years. Upright players especially. Not at all in an "ugly" way either but more in the way you'd look at a carpenter's hands or a landscaper's hands and think, "man, this guy has really put his 'time' in on his instrument." My hands actually have to work almost twice as hard as most because not only am I trying to play the instrument in all these ways, but they also have to find a way to prevent themselves from shaking from the ET. A lot of times that results in me either having to anchor my right hand in such a way on the bass so that it doesn't go into tremor as well as being conscious that my left hand doesn't cramp up from gripping the neck too hard. Playing with a pick does really help in a lot of ways as well as what I call a "modified" muted palm/thumb/1st, 2nd finger technique that I've been using. Something similar to what I've seen Sting use when he's playing bass.

Then there's times where my hands feel great, no tremors, no pain, nothing... than I can revert back to my typical two-finger, one finger per fret technique that I've used all along. I will say this too, BREATHING and RELAXING are essential in ALL of this. Like they say, if you don't breathe, you'll die.. LOL! There's obviously a lot of truth to that not just literally but in your playing. How many times do we get to a tough passage in our performance and we hold our breath as we try to get through it. I guess it's something we just do when we experience something painful or hard. I remember getting flu shots as a kid, or worse, stitches, and I would always hold my breath as the nurse would hit my arm with the needle. Same thing. Imagine if a horn player did that? They'd never get a note out! Point I'm making is to remember to breathe normally and relax! Enjoy the moment! Don't hold your breath!

Q: With your wealth of experience in many facets of playing and the industry, what mistakes from an injury prevention perspective do you notice most in a player's technique, or what conditions do you most see/hear about in players?

A: From a playing technique perspective, I think it would be posture and hand movement that I see a lot of players make mistakes in. I guess the word I'm looking for might be efficiency or efficiency in movement. Carpal tunnel syndrome was a term that was used quite a bit back when I was a student practicing 10-12 hours a day. I'm sure it's still prevalent in players today too. Look at a cat who wears their bass way low. Look at their fretting hand and the position their wrist is in. Crazy angles right? Then, on the other hand (no pun intended) look at a player who wears their bass too high and look at their plucking hand. Again, crazy wrist angles right? Then like I said, couple all of that with having a ten pound instrument strapped around your neck and shoulder all night... something will eventually break down after so many years of wear and tear. Add to all of this crazy stage performances, head-banging and jumping all over the stage, I think in a lot of ways we should be considered athletes!

The other thing I see a lot of guys do wrong doesn't even involve playing their instruments more so than it does transporting them! Face it, it's 2 a.m., you just finished packing up after a 4 hour gig. All you can think of is getting the hell outta the club and getting home. You're not thinking…"lift with your legs, not your back." Next thing you know, you're screaming in pain because you just tried to "muscle" your 8x10 cabinet into the back of your Toyota Corolla. Even the slightest "wrong" movement can put you out for weeks. This all pretty much translates into sore and in a lot of cases, injured shoulders, injured wrists (carpal tunnel), blown out backs and necks (disc damage). Heck, even your feet take a beating! I think the easiest way to prevent all of this is to make sure you're using good posture, both when lifting and carrying as well as performing. Consistently stretching your neck, back and shoulders, and warming your hands up before playing.

With my ET, I've found that if I warm my hands up, no matter how simple the gig is going to be, it REALLY helps to get the blood flowing. In the past, I would think, "oh man this is a really easy or low key gig, I'll be fine." Totally not the case anymore. I have to warm my hands up at least 10-20 minutes before I play anything. It not only helps reduce the effects of the ET during the show, but after the show my hands don't hurt. Stretching is also key! Making sure I stretch my lower back, legs, neck, shoulders… basically everything that can be stretched.

Last is proper diet. Again, let's face it, a lot of musicians I know don't always have the healthiest of diets. Running to gigs, quick stops through the drive-thru to pick something up. Then at the gig, couple of beers, couple of mixed drinks. Then there's the post gig 2 a.m. diner stop before going home. Multiply that times twice a week times 52 weeks a year. Not good. That all translates to how your body handles the abuse it takes ON the gig. Put junk fuel in your car, you're gonna get junk performance. Put the good stuff in and your car's gonna purr. Same thing with our bodies and our performances.

Q: Any special tips or general advice for players?

A: As just a broad brush stroke piece of advice… take care of yourself! I know I sound like an old fart when I say exercise, eat right and get plenty of sleep! Warm up before playing ANYTHING too! I know we don't all live in a perfect world so it's not always that easy to live by this motto but at least use it as a guideline. It doesn't matter how old or young you are either. If you're in this for the long run, slow and steady will always win the race.

Listen to what your body is telling you too. If your hands hurt after a gig, there's a reason for that. If your back is sore the next morning, there's a reason for that too. And don't just dismiss it as "getting older" or laugh it off as "old age". Man, my dad could kick my ass when he was in his late 60's. There's good pain and there's bad pain. Good pain is the feeling I get after a workout and my muscles are sore because I worked them hard. Bad pain is when my body is telling me, "hey, I'm injured, please don't DO that again." Learn to know the difference. And research what your body tells you as well. My ET got to be so frustrating that I started to research it not knowing what it was. Had I not done that, I would have never learned about ET nor would I have had it diagnosed and eventually been put on medication or found other remedies for it via social support groups.

Hope this helps in some small way to those reading this!

Peace, Dino

Thank You Dino!

Chi-chi Nwanoku OBE

Double bassist Chi-chi Nwanoku OBE studied at the Royal Academy of Music, where she is a Professor and Fellow, and with Franco Petracchi in Rome. She has been Principal bass player, chamber musician and soloist with many of Europe's leading orchestras. Chi-chi is the Founder, Artistic and Executive Director of the Chineke! Foundation, which encourages diversity in the classical music industry through its orchestras, the Chineke! Orchestra and Chineke! Junior Orchestra, and its community engagement work. Chi-chi has been instrumental in creating opportunities for talented Black and Minority Ethnic musicians through concerts, commissioning new works, championing historical BME composers, and by establishing scholarships with the major UK conservatoires.

She created the ABO/RPS Salomon Prize, which celebrates 'unsung heroes' working in the ranks of British orchestras. In 2012 Barrie Gavin directed a documentary film about Chi-chi's career, *Tales from the Bass Line* and in 2018 she featured on BBC Radio 4 *Desert Island Discs*. As a broadcaster Chi-chi has presented for BBC Radio 3 & 4, BBC TV Proms Extra, BBC 2 TV Classical Star, and BBC 4's *All Together Now, the Great Orchestra Challenge*. She also presented an award-nominated Sky Arts documentary profiling composer Samuel Coleridge-Taylor and hosted a Scala Radio show featuring guests from Chineke! Orchestra.

An Honorary Fellow of Trinity Laban Conservatoire and Honorary Doctor at Chichester University and the Open University, Chi-chi was awarded the OBE in 2017 for Services to Music. She has won Black British Business Awards 'Person of the Year'; an ABO Award for 'most important contribution to orchestral life of the UK'; the Commonwealth Cultural Enterprise Award for Women in the Arts and a Creative Industries Award at Variety Catherine Awards. Chi-chi has featured in the Top 10 of BBC Woman's Hour, Women in Music Power List, the Royal Academy of Music exhibition *Hitting the Right Note: Amazing Women of the Academy*, the 2019, 2020 and 2021. She is featured in the 2020 book of 100 Great Black Britons, and selected in the 100 Powerlist of Britain's 100 Most Influential Black People.

Q: As a double bassist, are there any specific problems or injuries you may experience on a regular basis or that you have experienced as a player? What did or do you do about these problems?

A: Injuries that I have experienced more than once during my career that have been purely through playing are: tennis elbow, golfer's elbow, neck ache/stiffness, low back pain/stiffness. More recently there was need for surgery on my right shoulder, due to 3 tendons having been very badly torn. The underlying cause for this was due to a small piece of 'extra bone' in my shoulder, that, were I not a classical double bassist, they may not have been torn. It was caused by the millions of bow reps over the years, bowing over the impingement of the bit of bone. The surgeon told me I had virtually been "sawing my way through my own tendons"!

Q: As a player who utilizes bowing in your playing, are there any special concerns to be aware of with this style regarding possible injuries that may occur?

A: I suspect it is always necessary to pay particular attention to over-gripping the bow, and to remember to transfer unnecessary tension and pressure away from the elbow area. To try and 'share the load' throughout the arm, back, wrist and fingers. Sometimes easier said than done!

Q: Are there any accommodations or changes in technique you may need to make in your approach to the instrument as a shorter player?

A: I believe playing positions are crucial whether you are tall or short. I think it is crucial to have my playing height as perfect as possible. That is, to ensure that I am not over-extended at any point of my body for any unnecessary length of time. Even down to the position and weight balanced between my feet. Shortly prior to my shoulder surgery, the only way I could play (using my bow) was by standing up. It meant I could bring the bass much closer to my body, and not have to reach forwards before bowing side-to-side! I had to learn how to stand and play, and got very used to it, but in the orchestra which sometimes involves playing a 4 hour Handel opera I was looking forward to being able to sit down again! The inevitable happened, in that post-surgery returning to my stool it felt much too low. Needless to say, I am still in the process of trying to recreate the optimum playing height that involves sitting on a stool. I have just had my stool modified, and it now stands at a height where I don't exactly 'sit' on it, but prop against it, slightly perched on the edge of the seat, and with my left foot on a yoga block! The jury is still out on that!

Q: Some players feel, male and female, that there are certain considerations due to strength that need to be made as a female bassist. As a female player, do you find this to be true and are there any particular considerations that need to be pointed out or made in this regard?

A: Not at all. Firstly, I believe there is nothing to be gained from sheer strength. In fact it can be a hindrance. I have seen massive, burly, macho people looking as though they are engaged in a boxing match when playing their instruments, and have been amazed at the puny, limited sound emanating from their instruments. At the opposite extreme I have seen slightly built people playing with a freedom and lightness, yet transmitting a natural weight beginning from their spine that travels through their entire arm through their fingers and into the bow, making twice the sound!

Q: Is there anything special that you do to get prepared for practice or performance, such as warm-ups or any other preparation?

A: If it is a day off (or a morning off) I usually try to go to the gym and do a little bit of strength and resistance work, rowing, lat pull downs etc. and some stretching, followed by a ¼ mile swim. It gives me a wonderful start to the day, getting all my circulation flowing, and I always feel lighter on my feet and ready for anything afterwards!

Q: What mistakes do you most notice in a student's or player's technique that could possibly lead to or contribute to future injury?

A: Sitting positions, height of instrument, bow holds.

Q: Any special tips, exercises or general advice you would like to share with players?

A: The exercises I still swear by are found in Petracchi's *Simplified Higher Technique*, for both left and right hand strength, dexterity and organized positions. Think of your instrument, and especially your bow as an extension of your voice. Find your unique language and voice, by listening and talking through your bow, rather than imposing yourself on it. You will soon find it is liberating both to yourself and the listener.

Thank You Chi-chi!

John Patitucci

John Patitucci needs hardly any introduction as one of the greats of the instrument. His ability to seamlessly move from electric to acoustic, from style to style with the greatest performers of our time is legendary. His solo work and work most notably with Chick Corea's Elektrik and Akoustic bands and the Wayne Shorter Quartet are essential listening for bassists and music fans alike. Visit him at www.johnpatitucci.com.

Q: Are there any specific problems or injuries you may experience on a regular basis or that you have experienced as a player? What did or do you do about these problems?

A: All my life I have had a strong constitution but I find at 61 years of age, especially in the last 5 years, I'm not 25 anymore. One big mistake with the double bass is that I sat for many years with one leg on the rung of the stool and the other on the ground, which would cause low back pain, but I continued, again, because of my strong constitution. I did this for many years and then finally began to stand more. Two years ago I did a bass concerto with both electric and double bass, and it was intense, not only the parts but playing with a chamber orchestra & I noticed some issues then. Also schlepping gear, and long practice sessions cause issues, playing too much, leaning over the instrument, the strap digging into the shoulder. I now will sit when I can while playing, with both feet planted on the ground. I learned all this the hard way, and changed playing strategies intuitively as I saw and felt what was happening. I still notice neck discomfort commonly from carrying gig bags, gear, etc.

Q: Are you aware of more problems playing double bass, or electric bass?

A: With the electric, I notice more problems behind the neck, this can be from pressing too hard on the fingerboard. When I was 13 years old my brother who played guitar went over my left hand technique with me and helped me to straighten everything out there, so that has been pretty good for me. Pressing too hard with the left hand can be a problem on the double bass, not only for the left hand but also the neck and shoulder, and bowing can be an issue.

Q: How much bowing do you utilize in your playing, and are there any special concerns to be aware of while bowing regarding possible injuries that may occur?

A: Yes I do a lot of bowing- and here's the deal: I played classical for many years, and started studying with John Schaeffer, who was the principal bassist for the New York Philharmonic and who played with Bernstein, etc., etc.. One thing he corrected immediately was that I was pressing too hard with my left hand on the neck creating tension there, and he taught me to use the weight of my arm rather than placing this stress on my thumb on the back of the neck. This in turn helped my bowing, as before I began to study with John I had learned from another teacher earlier to put my thumb on the stick with my right hand and not to bend it. This caused pain, but it worked and I was already successful with this technique so I just continued it. When I went to see John Schaeffer the next thing he corrected after the left hand was to have me put my thumb on the frog and to bend it, concentrating on the fulcrum and weight distribution between the forearm and the bow, similar to the left hand correction he had made with the weight of the arm. He also taught me to draw the bow without pressing, but rather use the weight of the forearm. He also taught students, young students in particular, that when you are ready for up bow, it is the arm which gives you weight, so simply move the bow with the arm. Having the elbow out and/or at an angle during the up bow is not good - keep it steady and again, simply move the bow with the arm.

Q: Do you play 4 & 5 string electric basses and if so are there any adjustments you make from one to the other and/or from them to the 6 string? What should a player be aware of when switching from a 4 string to a 6 string electric bass?

A: Placing and holding the thumb too tightly behind the neck creates problems and the width of the neck on the 6 string magnifies this. Also be mindful when string crossing- don't tense up with the right hand, and again watch the thumb behind the neck- it's too easy to hold on too tightly when trying to compensate for changes in the instrument and neck size.

Q: Any road or studio tips or routines you use to avoid injuries or problems?

A: Being aware of my body, not just being in my head, and noticing when things change and evolve. Musicians tend to live their whole lives inside of their heads. I have always found things out intuitively, such as if my right hand was bending at too much of an angle, I would change that. I remember playing these very intense electric gigs, and my chops were up and that wasn't a problem, and when I would go to play these particularly heavy passages in front of these audiences if my mind tensed up, my hands would also tense up. So my hands were ready, but my mind was not.

Q: Is there anything special that you do to get prepared for practice or performance, such as warm ups or any other preparation?

A: I always practice in the mirror. Warming up with the bow, I tend to practice long bow, and do arpeggios for pitch and shifting. With the electric I practice string crossing for groove playing, because if you haven't synced up your hands the rhythm suffers.

Q: What mistakes do you most notice in student or player's techniques, electric or upright, which may lead to short or long term problems?

A: With students I notice when sitting they may hunch over too much, so you need to watch your posture. If someone plays too long, say for 6 hours, in this position, they are going to be in a world of pain. With the left hand, the biggest problem is pressing too hard especially with the thumb on the back of the neck, as this can lead to hand pain, tendinitis, and arm pain. With the electric bass, many times players will hold the bass too low, this puts the right wrist at a bad angle and places too much tension on the right hand.

Q: Any special tips or exercises you would like to share with players?

A: Especially when bowing, don't approach the instrument to play with stiffness and tightness in your arms. No one walks around with their arms stiff at their sides, and one shouldn't play like that either. Pretend the bow is a chin-up bar, hold it over the head, hold it and then relax, curl the fingers around the stick, then bring it down and put it on the string, straight down without the elbow sticking out. Another mistake I used to make was thinking it was all in the wrist, when it's about the forearm; players are drawn to the wrist and the fingers and that 'big sound', but it's all in the forearm.

Thank You John!

Resources

Websites

Musicians

www.arianecap.com
www.bassmagazine.com
youtube BassWhispererTV
www.stuhamm.com
www.monotunesmusic.com
www.chi-chinwanoku.com
www.johnpatitucci.com

Author

www.drkertz.com
youtube drkertztv
Monthly videos at:
www.bassmusicianmagazine.com
www.drkertz.com
www.isbworldoffice.com
www.makingmusicmag.com

Products

www.gruvgear.com
www.fodera.com
www.sadowsky.com

Recommended Reading

The Bassist's Guide to Injury Management, Prevention & Better Health - Volume One
by Randall Kertz

Double Bass: The Ultimate Challenge
by Jeff Bradetich

The Evolving Bassist
by Rufus Reid

Randall Kertz is a chiropractic physician, acupuncturist, author, educator, lecturer, consultant and product developer for the music industry, and bassist in private practice in suburban Chicago, Il.. He treats many local, national and international musicians of all playing styles in his office, on tour, and via teleconference.

Made in the USA
Middletown, DE
21 September 2024